PROPERTY OF

_____

_____

CATHERINE JOHNSON was born in London, but her heritage is Jamaican and Welsh. She is a Fellow of the Royal Society of Literature and has written over twenty books for young readers, including *Race to the Frozen North* and *Freedom*. She also writes for film, TV and video games, everything from *Holby City* to *I Am Dead*. She lives by the sea in Hastings.

CATHERINE JOHNSON

A NEST of VIPERS

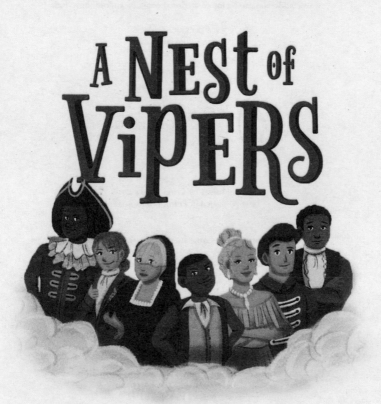

A PUFFIN BOOK

PUFFIN BOOKS

UK | USA | Canada | Ireland | Australia
India | New Zealand | South Africa

Puffin Books is part of the Penguin Random House group of companies
whose addresses can be found at global.penguinrandomhouse.com.

www.penguin.co.uk
www.puffin.co.uk
www.ladybird.co.uk

First published by Corgi Books 2008
First published in Puffin Books 2021
001

Text copyright © Catherine Johnson, 2008, 2021

The moral right of the author has been asserted

Set in 12.5/16.5pt Sabon LT Std
Typeset by Jouve (UK), Milton Keynes
Printed and bound in Great Britain by Clays Ltd, Elcograf S.p.A.

The authorized representative in the EEA is Penguin Random House Ireland,
Morrison Chambers, 32 Nassau Street, Dublin D02 YH68

A CIP catalogue record for this book is available from the British Library

ISBN: 978-0-241-51487-0

*This book is for my wonderful
grown-up daughters.*

Contents

1. Newgate Prison, London, September 1712

'HOW'D I come into the profession?' I was looking up at the priest in the dark of the condemned cell. I knew I was shivering – and not from cold either. In all my fourteen years I'd never been this close to death and it was only hours away. Hours until I was to hang. The priest knew that – he was smiling down at me through the gloom – and I had no intention of making his task a simple one.

The Newgate Ordinary, as the prison parson was known, pulled out a small stool and sat down.

'I know your game!' I said to him. 'You'll have this all down and sold on for some street ballad seller to sing in every square between here and Westminster before my body's cold!' I looked away, and would have walked away too, but the chains bit into my wrists and ankles. 'You'll call it "The Boy Who Made the *Favourite* Disappear!" Or "The Ship That Vanished" or some such nonsense!'

'The *Favourite*? Was that the name of the ship, the two-masted vessel, that clean vanished?' He tried to sound innocent.

'As if you didn't know!' I spat back at him.

'It's a long night,' the Ordinary said. 'The one before you hang. No one's called for you; there'll be no one in the mob to cut you down and save you from the surgeons! They'll hand you over and take their shilling piece. Think on that, lad. And we'd all like to know what happened to the vessel in question.' He coughed. I looked the other way in case he could read my face, even here in the dark. 'And the gold she had on board, of course. I mean, if there *was* anything you could tell me—'

'I'm no snitch! I'll tell you nothing!'

The Ordinary smiled. I shut my eyes. The dark of the condemned cell seemed just as black whether you had your eyes open or closed. And to tell the truth, I felt even more foolish because I was the only one of my 'family' to be caught for our crime. Indeed, to be caught for anything at all was bad enough . . . But to hang? That had to be nothing but my own stupidity.

The *Favourite*'s vanishing was to be Mother Hopkins's final act, her last hurrah before old age slowed her, and I had let her down . . . No wonder no one had asked for me.

I supposed my 'family', who were the nearest thing to blood relatives I could name, had vanished into the stew of the city. They must have reckoned me already good as dead. Mother Hopkins never even showed her face at my trial. I called her Mother – she taught me everything I know: reading, writing, the way to spring any lock you like – but she never bore me in the natural way. Paid threepence for me, she says, not that you can believe a word from her lips. I don't know why I should even care a fig for any of them.

But there's a lump in my throat feels like it's the size of a cannonball.

'*The* Mother Hopkins?!' the Ordinary asked. I nod, and his face lights up. 'I remember the woman myself! In here to swing like you, she was.

Not thirteen, fourteen years ago!' He rubbed his chin as if that action eased his memory. 'A fine-looking woman.'

I said nothing. Mother Hopkins – although possessed of many qualities, such as cunning and cleverness in parting a gentleman from his money without said gentleman realizing – would not, in my mind, be thought of as fine-looking.

The Ordinary sighed. 'Knew her well,' he said. 'Once.'

This was not a surprise. Mother Hopkins knew most of the useful people in London. I had heard the tale of how she escaped the condemned cell, and my infant part in that story (she would never have paid anything for me if I wasn't to be useful). But it seemed as though her devious ways would no longer be used to further my own little life.

None of the others had showed themselves. Not Bella, although to be honest I never expected to see her anyway. Sam Caesar and Jack Godwin were nowhere to be seen. Addeline came once, on the day the beak passed sentence. The judge wore his black cap as he brought down the hammer to end my short life. I saw Addeline and my heart leaped. She was up in the gallery, gripping the rail so hard her knuckles showed through like white marble. She was dressed as a boy, but I would know her anywhere, even though she never even looked down at me once. Just thinking about it now is bringing me close to tears ...

'So if you don't tell me, lad, who'll ever know?' The Ordinary's rough voice brought me back out of my dream. He took out his pen. 'Ah, go on then, son,' he urged. 'It's a good tale, I'll warrant! You should hear the ones they've made up about you already.'

'Oh?' I said, trying to sound casual, but he knew he had me hooked. 'What *do* they say about me?'

'They say the boat was magicked away by witchcraft! They say that you're too clever to be a boy, that you're a man who never growed, and that you had a sack of gold and you would walk about the streets by St Dunstan's throwing money in the air for poor children to catch.'

'Hah!' I would have folded my arms but the chains were so damn short they didn't allow for it. 'That was me and Addy once – we had so much cash in our pockets it was weighing us down. And we had to run so fast ...' I shook my head, remembering.

'They say you can escape from any lock save ones blessed by a bishop,' the priest continued. 'And that the vanished ship sails back and forth between the Indies and Africa, freeing slaves and causing pain for the planters!'

I smiled. 'Is that all?'

His eyes glinted in the darkness as he leaned towards me. 'And they say you're an angel that fell down into hell. That's on account of your smooth words, your kind eyes and your infernal skin.'

'My skin is far from infernal!' I protested. 'It's been my living every one of my fourteen years! I'm as proud of my colour as the peacock is of his feathers,' I said. 'Go on. Write that down to start.'

'So you'll talk?'

I took a deep breath. That was a big mistake because of the smell. The odour of the two others who were to hang with me tomorrow and the filth of us all packed together in sweat and grime filled my insides. It took me a long time to ready myself. How would I start? My education in crime, my life in and out of the Nest of Vipers (the best inn in London and that's God's truth), learning to pick a lock, and watching Addy turn over country gentlemen in Smithfield with her cards, playing Find the Lady?

Or the crime I was set to give my life for – the most incredible scam ever laid by man or woman: the secret of the *Favourite*? I smiled to myself. I'd keep some of my tales back a little longer.

Anyway, if I tried telling all, we'd run out of time and I would be swinging in the wind, dancing the devil's own jig on the end of a noose. There was so much to tell ... Arabella playing the fine lady; me, the page, done up like the Queen's Own dog's dinner. Or when I was younger, and Mother Hopkins sold me so many times over I almost forgot my own name. And we played so many lays over so many years – to be straight with you, it was just like any other line of work. But there were one or two times ... one or two marks who deserved absolutely everything they got. And, yes, one family stands out. In the end they were my own downfall – the Walkers of Greenwich.

Yes, I'd start there. And it was how we first met Sam Caesar. He's one of the best chairmen in town now, as it goes. Him and Jack Godwin rule Leicester Fields – they can carry you, in their sedan chair, from Covent Garden to St James's in half the time you'd make with a carriage and pair.

I only wished they were waiting for me now, outside, and I could slip my chains, melt into the walls and be away.

That wasn't going to happen. The judge was so afraid of me escaping again that I'm shackled and trussed like a pheasant in a butcher's window.

I looked at the Newgate Ordinary. He was so dirty you could only just make out his chaplain's collar. He was greedy for my words because to him they were solid old goree. Old goree? Blood and bread, quids, love-of-my-life, rhino ... *money*. The root of all evil and the staff of life. I made him promise he'd use some of the cash he'd get for my story to save my body from the surgeon's knife. Then I began.

'So, here they are,' I said, 'the last words of Cato Hopkins, boy criminal. Who only ever robbed those who were so greedy as to want more. Who only ever tried to share about the wealth of those who are fat with goods and silks and food—'

'Hold on!' the Ordinary said. 'Slow down, for the sake of my quill!'

I paused a while, then began again. 'It was like this. It was my eighth year or so; we was living above this public house, an inn just east of Drury

Lane: the Nest of Vipers. It was my home for longer than any other, but trade was slow and the only regular money coming in was from Bella's job at Two Crows coffee shop and whatever me and Addy brought in from the street. One day, not long after Whitsuntide, this boy walks in ... Well, he looked more like a man – he was the *size* of a man. It was Sam Caesar, fifteen but more than fully grown. He was bleeding from a knock on his head and he was so desperate it took more than Mother Hopkins's soft words and a cup of ale to quieten him down.

'"I need help," he said.

'Mother Hopkins dabbed away the blood and said, slow and not interested like: "I can see that, my lad. Now, what is it you think we can do for you?"

'He told us then about his owner, man name of Captain Walker, lived over Greenwich in one of them big new houses, stuffed to the gills with paintings and silver. Mother Hopkins's ears pricked up at this. But we'd already guessed as much, for the poor chap was wearing one of them god-awful silver collars that the rich put their slaves in. Have you seen them? Bet you've never worn one! They're the devil and that's the truth.

Heavy as lead, and there's nothing so likely to make you feel like a dog as wearing one of them. Sam's collar read: *SAM, Capt. Walker's Negro. Please return to Crooms Hill, Greenwich* in that curly writing. I felt a deal of pity for the boy just for that.

'Sam Caesar said he'd heard there was folk here who knew how to turn situations around, and his was a situation so parlous that he could not imagine any way out.

'So Bella put another cup of ale in front of the boy and smiled at him. If she hadn't been seeing Jack Godwin, she'd have set her cap at him, I'm sure of it. Sam Caesar was fine-looking – at least he would be when the gash on his head was cleaned up.

'Turned out Captain Walker had brought our Sam over from Jamaica when he was a lad. Captain Walker wasn't just a sea captain, oh no. He had a deal of estates in Jamaica producing sugar and rum. Owned hundreds of slaves, Sam said, and still owned his mother, Juno. Turns out she'd been a favourite with the captain – so favourite that Sam had a lighter skin than his mother, if you get my meaning. So favourite that she'd begged the captain to take Sam to London and give him some kind of education. So Sam had come over with the captain and grown up in Greenwich as their page; wearing one of them flashy outfits – slippers with those curly toes and a turban. Never learned nothing but serving chocolate and tea to visiting ladies, mind. Then a few years ago he'd grown too big for that lay and they used him as a footman. But the captain never liked him: any excuse and he'd get a clout like the one he was wearing today. And then he hears the captain's only gone and sold him to a mate and is having him shipped back to Jamaica on the *Retort* to be a field hand!

'I knew then why he trembled so. If you ever heard the old men in St Giles talking about life in the Indies, it would make your hair turn white. Floggings so hard flesh hangs in red ribbons from a man's back. Men, women and children worked until they break ... Arms, ears, tongues cut off! Death is your only friend out there, I've heard say, because it's a sleep you never have to wake from.

'So, already wanting to help, I said, "He wants to disappear." But Mother Hopkins shot me a *shut-up* look. "He's not free, Cato, not like you!" she said. "Someone'll buy him, sell him, in two shakes of a lamb's tail. He's not free, Cato," she said again.

'I said nothing. Mother Hopkins was always right. Whenever I was sold, usually in some town such as Nottingham or Derby or Bedford – once as far as Chester – we were up and had a distance of twenty miles between ourselves and my newest masters before they'd realized I had gone. And if anyone *was* foolish enough to come after me, Mother Hopkins had a tame lawyer – Mr De Souza in the Strand – with enough writs to confuse and confound our enemies. And failing that, Jack and Sam, who have more muscle than most . . . Anyway,' I said to the Ordinary. 'I am off the track of my tale and time is passing . . . What was I saying?'

The priest squinted hard at his paper. 'You were talking of this Sam, and the matter of being free . . .'

'That sounds like it. And wouldn't I give anything for a little bit of that selfsame freedom.'

The Ordinary glared at me.

'I know, I know, this is Sam's tale, and I can see him, in my mind's eye, fair jump up out of his seat at the mention of liberty. "Free!" he said. "Captain Walker promised my mother he'd make me a free man. I was there when he made the promise, and she gave him a letter! She put it into his hand the day I left. He denies it all, of course, says my mother could hardly speak English, let alone read and write. They never bothered teaching me, so I can't tell. I found a bundle of letters but they all look the same – black lines on white paper, like the trails of ants or some such."

'After Sam's outburst Mother Hopkins thought a long minute. "So this man owes you at least your freedom?" Sam nodded. "And he has plenty of rhino about the house?" she asked him. Sam looked blankly at her, which was no surprise given where he'd come from. So Mother Hopkins said, "Rhino, ready money, cash?"

'Sam understood then and nodded again. "His wife is most fond of the cards, though she loses as often as she wins, and she has jewellery too – they have so much money from the backs of their slaves, who work day and night for them but are paid nothing!" I tell you, Sam was so angry when he spoke, it was hard for him to keep still. "But whatever plans you make, it must be soon," he said. "I am to leave his household in a fortnight, and go to Rotherhithe, where the boat will be loaded."

'Now, Mother Hopkins seems to sit at the heart of a web that stretches all over the city. She had Addy go over to Greenwich to check out the gaff, and Bella went to some rather genteel card games with her pockets full of flummery – fake cash to you – where she picked up a not inconsiderable amount of info. I was to be the inside man, although as I was just eight, I suppose you would say *boy*. But I had done the job so many times before, I was no bother. Bella let slip there was a sale in Long Acre. Mother Hopkins had the bills produced:

'FOR SALE: CATO, A MOST PLEASANT AND AGREEABLE NEGRO BOY OF ONLY SIX YEARS OF AGE, they said (I know, I was eight – never believe any advertisements ever). NEW FROM THE JUNGLES OF ZANZIBAR, HE IS A MUTE, HAVING BEEN RAISED BY LEOPARDS! (What did I say about advertisements?)

'Mother Hopkins knew it would hook the captain's wife. Sam had told us she was looking for a new page, and that she wanted one more exotic and more mysterious than Mrs Gerald's boy, of whom it was said – mostly by Mrs Gerald herself – that he had been found floating in the Indian Ocean in a giant shell.'

The Ordinary smirked as he continued to write, his quill scratching across the page furiously. I had no idea how he could see anything in this gloomy light.

'I always hated the sales. We had played this game so many times before – me the slave, sold by Mother Hopkins, over and over all around the country, and I never stayed in any of them fine houses longer than a fortnight . . . There's another hundred more tales for you, sir! I know, I know, I must keep to one story at a time.

'So, even though in my heart of hearts I knew I would be back at the Nest of Vipers within the week, there was something about the saleroom that made my eye moisten and my lip tremble every single time. Mother Hopkins encouraged this as she said it made a good spectacle.

'Captain Walker was a nasty piece. I could tell this by the way he checked my teeth as if I was a horse, prodding around inside my mouth so hard I could not help but flinch. I was much minded to bite off his fingers, but Mother Hopkins fixed me with her evil eye. He paid five guineas for me, then he took me straightway by boat to Greenwich, and Addeline was right: the house was one of those big show-off white-icing affairs.

'It is strange that people who wouldn't dream of walking through the streets with their money hanging out of their pockets are more than happy to advertise their wealth through clothes or carriages or houses. Don't you agree, sir? The house gleamed like a beacon to the cracksmen of London, and I thought they would have fine pickings here.

'I tell you, my jaw fairly dropped when I got inside. Paintings – ships and portraits mostly (I would ignore the portraits; they never sold) and one of horses in the modern style that Mother Hopkins would be most pleased with. I reminded myself to keep my hands hard in my pockets, though, for our spoils were to be human rather than material.

'Then Mrs Walker comes down the stairs clapping her hands and saying, "Oh! Oh! He is a darling, and he is mute, John? Such a fetching affectation!" Then the captain says to her, "He'll do. At least he'll be quiet. How is Elizabeth? Did she like the Stapleton lad? His father is a marquess: we could not do better."

'So the missus says, "Oh yes, John, she's quite taken with the diamond necklace he bought her. And all that dreadful business can be forgotten.

They're coming round for tea this afternoon and now little Sam here can do the honours in his fine suit." She claps her hands together again. "What a pet!" she coos, chucking me under the chin, and says to me very slowly, as if she reckons I can't understand the Queen's English: "You'll be our Sam now – the name's on the collar and we're not about to change it. We've always had a Sam here and we always will." She leans down to me and her eyes are pale and watery and she says, "You'll find Greenwich a deal of difference to the jungle, little Sam." I have to bite my tongue hard to stop myself laughing out loud. And she leads me away to put on the threads I am to spend my working week in.

'The suit is brocade, navy blue and also heavy as lead and the turban too big. Mendes, the cove that Mother Hopkins sells old threads to, would give a pretty penny for the lot but they don't half itch. And the collar! Wouldn't you know it is the same one Sam had been wearing the week before, so it is far too big and digs into my shoulders a good deal.

'At least I am right good at pouring chocolate from a silver pot. Mother Hopkins has taught me well. And I see the daughter, Miss Elizabeth – well,

I see her sparklers, which are as beautiful as she is, only more honest-looking, and I'm so busy thinking about how Mother Hopkins would die of delight if she could see that necklace that I forget to serve the visitors – Lady Stapleton and her lumpy son.

'"Sam!" Mistress Walker chucks me under the chin. I do nothing for a long minute on account of having forgotten I'm now Sam and not Cato. "Sam, our guests!" Then she says to Lady Stapleton, "He is newly come from Africa, directly from the jungle ... He doesn't speak a word ..." She looks at me with mock pity. "Captain Walker says he is the son of a prince and was brought up by leopards!"

'I stood up straight, and I would have laughed if Miss Elizabeth hadn't been pinching me hard – to see if I'd squeal, I reckoned. I had to feel pity for the girl – there she was being lined up for the Stapleton boy, just like me at the auction. I looked hard at him. It would not be a barrel of laughs being married to him. But at least her collar was made of diamonds, and she did not seem to mind. I think she was set on his fortune, not on his looks or manners, and in view of her pinching, her manners were of the same rank as his.'

I paused, trying to make myself more comfortable, although that was impossible. My final hours were no luxury.

'Sam had been put to work in the garden and bade not to leave the house or grounds. I could see him through the window, turning over the cold earth. He ate with us in the kitchen but as I was supposed to be mute, nothing was ever said. He was nervous though, I could tell.

'At night I slept down in the kitchen and talked to Sam then. I sprang the lock on my collar – they insisted I sleep in it – and resolved to take Sam's letter. I tiptoed back up the stairs to the study. The lock was feeble and the door opened easily, as did Captain Walker's bureau. Inside, however, there were so many letters I lost all faith that I would find it ... Letters from moneylenders and ships' companies, sums of money flying back and forth across various oceans and through various banks. But eventually I came across the very same. It was *written on behalf of a Mistress Juno Walker of Spanish Town, Jamaica, by the Reverend Butler.* Juno, I thought to myself – Sam's mother. I knew the fashion for giving us darker-skinned people such fanciful names as have come out of legends or history. For example, Cato is not – as Addeline would tease me – the king of Cats – but the finest Roman that ever lived. Although as you see, sir, I am not myself a Roman, and neither, I expect, was this Juno, who probably had a priest write for her and, by her words, beg that her son should be treated better than she was. And Walker? Well, don't most slaves wear their masters' names, whether or not they wish to?

'Back to the letter . . . The writing was faded and old. I held it up to the window where the moonlight streamed in over Greenwich Park and thanked Mother Hopkins for teaching me the reading as I reckons that sometimes it is more valuable and just as useful as the best set of lock picks money can buy.

'The next few days dragged as slow as the Cheapside night watchman, and he has such a limp that he can hardly make it down St Paul's Churchyard. The household was busy enough: Captain Walker with his shareholdings, Mistress and Miss Walker with the wedding that had been brokered with the Stapleton family. I stood in the corner of the drawing room with my silver tray, saying nothing. They treated me much as they would a lap dog: from the mistress it was soft words, from Miss Elizabeth pinches, and from the captain slaps and kicks. I felt sorry for Sam having such a father and was glad I had none. I was looking forward to the day I could walk out of their house and take off the torturous silver collar for good. I was only sorry I wouldn't see the look on the captain's face when he realized what was happening.

'I busied myself with secreting little things they wouldn't miss: a hatpin with a pearl, a couple of silver spoons, and the captain's seal, which he used for business correspondence. I tossed them all over the wall when I knew Addy was waiting by the park, as a little taster. I threw the letter over too, knowing Mother Hopkins would make the best use of it and that Sam would like to see his mother's letter when this was all over.

'The captain noticed his seal gone that evening. He was like an ox that's been driven wild at Smithfield by the 'prentices, and made the same amount of noise and mess, throwing his papers about and bellowing. The mistress was obviously well used to this behaviour. She told him it had probably been just misplaced or, worst of all, fallen down between the boards, and not to go so red in the face. His anxiety would be the death of him, she said, and made Miss Elizabeth sing to soothe him, which I think only made him worse.

'That night Sam came to me where I slept in the kitchen. He was almost mad with worry and fear. "They are coming for me in the morning, Cato! And I have seen no progress! I can wait no longer – I will run tonight. You can open the front door for me and I can take a place on a boat."

'I begged him not to go. Captain Walker would know all the boats this side of the river and probably half the ones on the north side. So I pleaded with him: "Sam, please! You must trust Mother Hopkins. Captain Walker will put a price on your head if you run, and any boat man will turn you over soon as look at you!"

'"You are but a baby who knows nothing!" he said, and I made to speak again but Mrs Leppings the cook came to see what the noise was. I stayed up all night in case I heard him try to leave. I was so vexed I bit my fingernails to the quick imagining Sam chained to the mast of a boat in the Thames and – in my worst nightmares – me alongside him, sailing for the plantations.'

The Ordinary stopped writing to rest his hand. He stared at me through the bleak light, no doubt guessing I would rather be heading for the plantations than heading for the noose. Both options were hell, but one was a living one. I shifted uncomfortably and he picked up his quill once more.

'So,' I continued, sighing, 'in the morning the doorbell sounded at eight thirty, and Sam was shaking. But it was a messenger from the bank, a boy dressed in the livery of the Commonwealth and Indies Trading Bank. A slight and slender boy, but the captain let him in and the boy winked at me. I had to keep my face straight because Addeline made such a very convincing boy.

'She asked for the captain's signature and waited while he signed and sealed (with his second-best seal) various letters. Then the messenger boy was gone. So when (I imagine) the Mistress Walker called for her little Sam to pour chocolate that morning at eleven, she called for ever, louder and louder and longer and longer until she must have been quite red in the face. Sam and I had slipped out of the back door into the street, where Mother Hopkins and Bella waited with a change of clothes for me, and Sam Caesar's certificate of freedom signed and sealed that morning by the captain himself. By eleven o'clock me and Sam were sat snug in the upstairs room at the Nest of Vipers,

Mother Hopkins counting the cash she'd made from selling my collar and clothes, Addy still dressed as a boy, her eyes saucer-wide as I told her about the house and the diamonds.

'I read Sam the letter from his mother, her tender words hoping her son would find his freedom in England, but Sam snatched it away, pretending the tears I could see so plain were provoked by nothing but a bit of dust. Oh, I should mention, Sam can read himself now. Bella taught him, and Mother Hopkins bought the fine sedan chair he runs with Jack Godwin – you must have seen them, all in their wigs and livery. You won't find sharper pair of young men! I had hoped, one day' – I sighed and shifted on the hard stone floor – 'that I would be like Sam.'

I tried to stretch – my wrists were raw and oozing under the shackles – and yawned, making the Ordinary yawn too. He was still scratching away with his quill. Then, when I spoke no more, he looked up from his scribbling and said, 'Was that the end of it? Didn't the captain come after you? What about the sparklers – the diamonds? I thought you were going to pocket them? And how does this relate to the *Favourite*, boy? Was that not tied into the Walkers? Wasn't that the captain in court done up in naval rig?'

'Perhaps,' I said. 'And we had his seal, remember, and a lot more besides. And the sparklers . . . Well, that'll be another story.'

I could tell from the tone of his voice that the Ordinary fair drooled to hear more. Outside the watchman called the hour for five o'clock. I had so little time . . .

We'd be leaving at ten for the drive to Tyburn along the Oxford Road and then the hanging, my hanging, at noon.

I closed my eyes and let out a deep breath. Only seven more hours . . .

2. A Fleet Wedding, Winter 1711

THE PARSON reeked of spirits. Cato had heard Mother Hopkins promise him as much of the best Geneva as he could neck if the ceremony was over before ten. Cato thought this a good plan on account that they would all freeze if the ceremony took any longer. It was cold as ice, even with the tiny fire sputtering yellow flames in the grate.

Cato thought that the debtors who were forced by law to live within the Liberty of the Fleet could probably only afford very small fires, another reason for offering cut-price, ask-no-questions marriage ceremonies. And 'Liberty' was, in truth, the worst word to give to what was essentially a wall-free prison – a prison of streets and houses and inns and shops. It was to be marvelled at that the prisoners could find the cash for even a few coals. Mother Hopkins said the Liberty of the Fleet had come about because the local prison had no more room, and debtors, being punished for their lack of money rather than their use of violence, were told to live as close as possible to the prison, if not actually inside it.

The parson swayed slightly as he pronounced the couple man and wife. The groom, Lord Peters's first and only son, Edgar, shone with bliss, and Bella, bride for a third time in six months, tried her best to look at least pleased, if not authentically smitten with love's arrow. Her blonde curls were pinned in the latest style and she was quite the picture dressed in Spitalfields silk and garlands of ivy.

Mother Hopkins cried real tears of joy, but Cato imagined she was not thinking of the couple's future life of matrimonial happiness but the guineas she would squeeze from Lord Peters to engineer a way out of the union for his son. Her own hair had been that shade of yellow once, she'd said. But now it was salt-and-pepper grey and hidden under a widow's veil.

Cato picked up the fiddle as the bride and groom signed the register. His fingers were so cold he wondered if the tune would come out straight at all.

Mother Hopkins waited until the ink was set and blotted, and then nodded at Cato, who struck up 'No Truer Love' with all the energy he could muster. Addeline, listening downstairs, would hear her cue and come dashing up the wooden stairs, red in the face as if she'd run all the way from Piccadilly to warn our groom to return home at once in case the wedding was discovered. The groom would usually hesitate – after all, the adjoining bedroom had already been booked for the evening – but Mother Hopkins could usually get him downstairs and into a chair for home in five minutes.

Sure enough, Addeline came heavy booted up the stairs, wearing her boys' jacket and squashed and dusty old tricorn hat. Cato could swear there was more than one footfall but he was concentrating on a difficult place in the tune, and then suddenly Addy was there, red-faced, agitated, wringing her hat in her hands for an instant before she was pushed aside by a man as big as the door frame.

The pistol shot made the parson faint. He dissolved into a pool of black fustian cloth. Cato dropped his fiddle and felt Addy grab his hand and throw him to the floor.

'Get down!' she hissed.

Two men had followed her up. From the buckles on their shoes – silver; Cato reckoned Mendes would give them plenty for either set – they were wealthy. He heard Mother Hopkins coughing, and when he looked, one had a sword at Bella's throat. It was right up against the skin and Cato could see her veins pulsing and her chest heaving and he wanted to stand up and push the man aside, because even though it was Bella, who would sometimes tease him or ignore him, she did not deserve that. One move and the blade was through her skin!

But Addy, seeing the look in his eye, held him down and whispered, 'Cato! No! It is Lord Peters and his man!'

'Father! Please!' Edgar tried to stand between the swordsman and Bella.

'Father?' Lord Peters spat out the word as if it tasted rotten. 'You still have the nerve to call me that!' He turned to Mother Hopkins, who in the absence of the parson – still out stone cold on the floor – was the most senior person in the room.

'You! Crone! Is this your doing? I cannot believe he –' he pointed at his son, now shaking and pale as Bella's silks – 'could be part of such devilry without some assistance!'

Mother Hopkins glared at Lord Peters so hard, Cato thought she would spit fire, but when she spoke, it was softly, gently.

'Sirs, please. Put down your arms. We are but women and children here.'

Cato flinched. He and Addy were no children. He was thirteen at the last count and Addy roundabouts twelve, both most definitely old enough to look after themselves.

Lord Peters nodded at the swordsman, who then lowered his blade. Bella swooned slightly. Her new husband gallantly held her up.

'Step away from the trollop!' Lord Peters thundered.

'She is not a trollop!' In comparison with his father's, Edgar Peters's voice was thin and reedy, and Cato saw that he was only a year or two older than himself. Next to him Bella looked every inch a grown woman. Edgar Peters was most definitely a boy. Cato felt sorry for the lad, and there was another feeling, a tingling that he knew was not just the cold. Shame, perhaps.

'She is my wife! We are in love!' Edgar Peters stamped his foot.

'Stupid boy! In love? You are sixteen! Sixteen! And besides, what has marriage to do with love?' Lord Peters turned back to Mother Hopkins. 'Well? How much did you want? How was it to be, the price to escape this tawdry union? A guinea a month in perpetuity or a lump sum when we arrange his real wedding – although what woman would want this excuse for a son I cannot say. Well, crone, speak!'

'I am not a crone,' Mother Hopkins said with dignity. 'And my daughter Arabella is as fine a girl—'

'Cut to the chase, woman! This is the Liberty of the Fleet, the biggest open prison and open sewer in all London. This is not St Paul's! A marriage here is a marriage far from prying eyes or society. It's hardly a marriage at all! Don't tell me this was any more than a sham, a beau trap!'

Mother Hopkins gasped theatrically. Cato, watching, thought she would have made an excellent actress. Lying seemed to come so easily to her.

Lord Peters sighed. 'For pity's sake, woman. I am not a fresh-faced country bumpkin with no knowledge of the city or people like you. Now, business. I will give you five guineas to burn the register.'

'Father, no! I love her! You shall not part us!' Edgar pleaded.

Mother Hopkins said nothing. Bella moved away from her husband and nearer to the fire.

'Bella!' Edgar Peters looked longingly at his wife and Cato felt even sorrier for him.

'Five guineas, and if you keep me waiting any longer, I will burn the damn register myself and my man here will let his sword do the work on you and your daughter.'

Mother Hopkins took a deep breath. 'Then I will see your money first, sir!'

'Madam, no!' Edgar looked at Bella. 'My love! They can't do this. Our union has been blessed!'

'You'll thank me for this in time.' Lord Peters called his man over. 'Hughes, take Edgar down to the carriage. At once.'

The swordsman took Edgar by the arm and led him away from his wife. He didn't go quietly as he was dragged down the stairs. 'Bella! Please, I will always love you, Bella! Always!' Cato could hear him shouting from the street.

Bella turned away and regarded herself in the mirror by the fireplace. Cato wanted to shake her. She could at least have been kinder, seemed a little more concerned.

Lord Peters passed a purse to Mother Hopkins. Cato knew she could tell the contents of a purse without ever looking inside it. She weighed it in her hand and a second later had torn the page from the register and watched as it curled to nothing in the flame.

'Good.' Lord Peters looked from Bella to Mother Hopkins. 'I will be more than happy if I never see either of you again. And if I do, you can guarantee I will not be so restrained with my pistol. Good day.'

No one moved or said anything until the carriage had gone. Cato stood up and rubbed a peep hole in the frosted window to make sure.

Bella threw her wedding garland into the fire. 'I swear, that is the last time I am getting married! Do you know how scared I was?'

Mother Hopkins tipped the purse on to the table and counted out the five guineas. 'You're not getting any younger, Bella, that's for certain.'

'Mother!' she said and Addy laughed, more out of relief than anything else, Cato thought.

He watched as the carriage turned the corner and disappeared into the traffic on Turnmill Street. 'I do not think we should play the mock wedding any more,' he said. 'That poor boy. He has a broken heart.'

'Ooh, Cato,' Bella said. 'You will find out in a year or so that broken hearts are ten a penny!'

'She is right, Cato,' Mother Hopkins said. 'And anyway, better a broken heart than one that has never known love. He will remember Bella for ever and will think constantly of her kisses for at least a week, a month maybe. He will fall in love again, and it will be truer and deeper and . . . and all that rubbish you find to sing about in those songs and poems of yours.'

They were mocking him, Cato knew that. He also felt sore and aggrieved that Mother Hopkins and Arabella could treat love so lightly. He doubted that either of them really knew what love was if they could let it go the way they did. Cato thought he ought to warn Jack that Arabella was not as constant as she pretended when she sat on his lap by the fire at home.

The parson stirred and pushed himself up from the floor shakily. 'Fetch the Watch! Call the Watch! We are dead! All dead! By pistol fire delivered over to the other side!' He looked at Cato. 'My God, the devils in hell are blacker than sin!'

'Parson Langley.' Mother Hopkins shook him hard by the shoulders. 'You are no more dead than I. This is not hell, this is Frying Pan Alley and out there –' she held his face up to the window – 'is St Paul's Cathedral, and this –' she turned him back to face Cato – 'is my own dear son, not a devil from hell nor any one of Satan's imps.'

As they walked home, the snow began falling. Bella had gone in a chair to save her dress from the slush in the street that blackened everything it touched. Mother Hopkins pulled her shawl close and Addy and Cato slipped and slid through the rubbish of Holborn Hill westward to the inn on Great Queen Street. Mother Hopkins was quiet and Cato could tell she was thinking. He knew she was worrying, though – five guineas from the wedding scam wasn't enough. But at least they all lived and breathed and they'd eat until the end of the week.

Cato watched Addeline and hoped she wouldn't grow up as fickle and careless as Bella. She ran ahead round a corner and Cato thought she could never care as much for clothes and presents as

Bella. Not Addy. He was thinking this as he turned the corner and she hit him full face with a snowball, which exploded stinging ice crystals down inside his clothes and all over his body.

'Addy, you devil!'

'Aye, and you one and the same!' she shouted back as she ran off.

Cato scooped up a handful of snow in his tingling hands. He aimed it for the centre of her back and got her just before she ran into the inn.

The sign was heavy with snow and the picture on it was hard to make out. It was a knot of snakes writhing in and out of each other and the words THE NEST OF VIPERS was marked out in red. Home, thought Cato, and what's more, home to the best gang of coney catchers, thimble twisters, sly coves, or any of the hundreds of names that confidence tricksters go by, in the whole of London town. Cato couldn't remember any other kind of life. Mother Hopkins was as good as any real mother, he supposed; he had good shoes and enough clothes even for this cold weather.

In the bar the regulars sat close to the fire. Ezra Spinoza, the massive ex-boxer who ran the bar with Sally, his wife, smiled as Cato and Addy

went past. Cato loved The Vipers: he'd lived here nigh on half his life and it felt as comfortable and as warm as the sheepskin he kept on his bed. The walls were washed with white lime, turned yellow by the fire and countless tobacco pipes. There were pictures on the wall of Mother's choosing: a horse that she claimed had won her enough money to buy the lease on The Vipers; a pale, dark-eyed young man she swore blind was Bella's father; and the cliffs down by the sea at Kent, where she said her childhood was passed finding ways to escape the sea and the smell of fish, and seek her fortune in the city. And there were the pictures the Spinozas had added: one engraving of Ezra in his heyday, fighting Rowley George, the Irish Terror, and another of him beating Toby Forewood, the Marquess of Abingdon's favourite. Cato loved the one of Ezra and Rowley a good deal and had spent many hours marvelling at the muscles on the young Ezra Spinoza in the picture.

Upstairs in the comfortably appointed drawing room above the bar, Bella had already changed out of her wedding gown, and brought them up hot mulled wine and fresh bread rolls from the bakehouse in Drury Lane. Bella was Mother

Hopkins's only blood relative. Well, Cato told himself, the only one they knew about. Mother Hopkins wasn't exactly old, but she had the wisdom of someone who had lived nearer one hundred years than the forty or so she admitted to.

Mother came up a good half-hour later. She had changed back into her usual, less showy widow's blacks but her face was set hard. Cato knew something was up because Sam Caesar and Jack were there too. They were all there, all of Mother Hopkins's professional family: Bella, the beauty, blonde ringlets and pink cheeks; Jack and Sam, strong and quick and ready if muscle was needed; Addy, her light brown hair untidily tied off her face, comfortable in her boys' britches; and Cato, almost as tall as Jack but not as broad, with nimble fingers from picking locks and playing the fiddle.

Mother Hopkins took her place in the good over-stuffed chair that was closest to the fire and her face was lit by the fierce orange firelight. Cato thought that he could see how Bella would turn out one day from the set of her face. She was still handsome, but you could never tell exactly what she was thinking purely from looking at her.

Mother Hopkins sat up and cleared her throat. 'Chickens, I am too old for London, too old for scams and schemes. Today was too close a shave.'

Cato looked at Addy and he knew she was thinking the same thing: how could you be too old for anywhere?

She went on, 'There must be change. I am too well known and my actions are anticipated. It seems to me that the good people of London watch me harder every day.'

'Mother, do not worry so,' Addy said. 'When Bartholomew Fair opens in the summer, there will be pickings for all of us – stupid farm boys, and stupid farmers with more money than sense.'

'Addeline, I am grateful for your kind thoughts but I am getting old. I do not want to live my final years dependent on greedy farmers who think they can beat you at cards or on wedding scams that go wrong. Someone could have been hurt today.' Mother looked at Bella.

Everyone was quiet. Someone *was* hurt today, Cato thought, remembering poor Edgar with his broken heart.

'You are my family, chickens. You know that.' Mother Hopkins looked around the room. 'And

I would not go without any one of you. So . . . we must have a plan.'

Addy leaned forward. 'What kind of plan, Mother?'

Mother nodded as though she had been thinking about this for some time. 'A big one, Addy. One so big that no one would ever think it possible. One that would net us enough old goree to never lift a finger or pick a pocket or play cards ever again. I want to buy us a house, like the quality do. A big house, with enough rooms, well appointed . . . in the country maybe.' She sighed. 'No more watching my back, forever wondering if the magistrate's men will have me.'

Jack Godwin whistled. He leaned forward and his chestnut hair shone in the firelight. 'That would take a deal of cash, Ma. And me and Sam, as things stand, we can make an honest wage. Life is good for us here. I don't mean to disrespect you, Mother, but we don't need to get involved in anything dodgy. Not now we own the chair outright. Thing is, me and Sam, we're on the straight an' narrow – the law don't give us no trouble now, Ma . . .'

Mother Hopkins looked furious. 'And how did you come by the readies to purchase said chair?

Answer me that! From the backs of Addy and her cards or Cato and his bag of lock picks! You are a part of this and never forget it! How did Sam here come to be your partner? Providence? Hah! More work than you care to think of, and none of it straight! Sam at least owes us his very freedom and you, Jack Godwin, would have been thrown on to the mercy of the parish if I hadn't taken you under my wing! What was it they were to do with you? Oh yes, you were to be pressed into service – one of the prettiest cabin boys in the Pool of London, and don't we all know what happens to them!'

Cato saw Jack's face flush scarlet.

'But the country is so dull, Mother!' Arabella pouted.

Mother Hopkins looked into the fire. 'I am thinking of Bath. There's enough parties and the like to keep you happy, and Jack and Sam could wipe the floor with the West Country chairmen. You would clean up, I warrant!'

'Bath!' Arabella smiled. 'That's a different kettle of fish! I have heard the season in Bath rivals London!'

'Bath?' Addeline looked unconvinced. 'I like London.'

Cato looked at Addy and agreed. He liked London too. But he knew how afraid Mother Hopkins was of Newgate. She had escaped the hangman once, in her youth, but Tyburn on a hanging day made her fearful. The only time he'd seen Mother Hopkins shake was when the cart for the gallows at Tyburn passed and the poor wretches ready for the off blew kisses and waved to the crowd on the Oxford Road.

And Newgate smelled of death. Cato always tried to avoid the bulky dark stone building, going the long way round just to avoid the sight of it. But if the wind was in the wrong direction, it would carry the scent of death and dirt and men shut up, and blow it right into your face. Bath must be a thousand times better than Newgate, he thought.

'Bath will be an adventure,' Cato said aloud to reassure Addy as much as himself.

Sam agreed. 'A new start, a new challenge.'

'But we have a lot to do,' Mother Hopkins said. 'And we'll need more money, more blood and bread than we've ever even sniffed at before.' She shifted in her seat and put the palms of her hands out to catch the best of the warmth from the fire.

'I've not decided on the lay. We need to choose our mark first then cut the plan to fit our mark closer than a brocade waistcoat. Someone with more money than brain and enough of a hunger for wealth that he will do anything to grab extra cash.'

'Mayfair and St James's is full of them,' Jack said. 'They ride our chairs and talk of South Sea investments and slaving and tobacco and sugar as if the money is lying on the ground in the colonies and all you have to do is get your servant to bend down and pick it up for you.'

'It's stocks and shares that are the thing, Mother. The lottery has had its day but the rich love to speculate,' Sam said.

'Speculate?' Addy said. 'Bet? Like on the horses?' She pulled her jacket close and listened.

'Exactly so,' Sam told her. 'I heard Lord Adeney's son bet one hundred pounds on which of his satin slippers would wear out the fastest!'

'You lie!' Addy said, open-mouthed.

Mother Hopkins clapped her hands. 'Enough! We will need to study harder than the scholars up in Oxford for any plan to work. Tomorrow, Bella, find yourself a place at one of those coffee shops frequented by gentlemen. Find one where trade is the thing, not politics or books. Sam and Jack, keep your ears and eyes open! Who is spending money like there's no tomorrow? Big amounts mind – thousands, not hundreds!'

'And us, me and Addy?' Cato asked.

Mother Hopkins looked from one to the other.

'I am almost as tall as Jack!' Cato said.

Jack laughed.

Mother Hopkins thought. 'You'll to St James's and see who's moving into the new houses around Green Park. Watch and listen, chickens. Watch and listen.'

Cato could see Addy's head droop and Mother Hopkins must have seen it too.

'Addeline, Cato. This is the long game we must play. And if you will play the long game, you must work hard and keep quiet, look hard and say little. We are not playing for odd pennies here and there! If you are not yet old enough to take a part, then I would rather you stayed out of this.'

She looked hard at them both and Cato knew she was right. Addy was good at the street game, the Find the Lady card booth; she had once taken a whole guinea that way at Smithfield Market. But a house in Bath would take planning.

'I know that, Mother,' Addy said. 'Cato and me will do what's needed.'

'I know you will. I know you all will.' Mother sat back in her chair. 'So find me a good mark. A fleshy mark, a soft and greedy mark, one who'll think we'll give him the world on a plate and that he deserves it. It's always better – always easier – to rob a dishonest man, a lying man. Then what we do is less a crime against society but more of a favour, a redistribution of wealth, you might say.'

'Like Robin Hood in stories. Giving to the poor!' Addy said. Cato could see that taking a big mark was getting them all excited, even Addy.

'So find us a lazy mark,' Mother continued. 'One that lies as often as he opens his mouth, one with a mistress or two maybe, one who loves money more than his own children's life. One who deserves to live in penury and know a hunger for bread and such cold as he can only dream of!'

Mother Hopkins spoke with such fury, Cato imagined she must have felt that hunger herself more than once. The others were quiet. The log spat in the fire and Mother Hopkins relaxed. She sat back in her chair, smiled and closed her eyes like a cat with a plate full of fish tails. 'And then we will take him for every last penny he has!'

3. A Walk Up West

'I HAD SO wanted to see the Frost Fair today.'
Addeline was sulking. Cato could feel it in the
drag of her step. He put his arm through hers.
The cold was bitter and their breath escaped in
huge clouds of vapour.

'The Thames will not melt overnight, Addy.
There will be plenty to see tomorrow. In fact,
unless spring comes in January, there will be
plenty to see until next February!'

'Cato, you are too sensible,' she said. 'Bella has
been already!'

'And bought enough fairings and fancies to fit
out a troupe of acrobats!' Cato exclaimed.

'She saw them, the acrobats. And she said they
were from Spain, wearing orange and gold, and

46

leaping and turning so fast! You should like them, I'm sure.'

Cato agreed. 'I never said I wouldn't, although how they will keep their hands from fixing to the ice with cold is beyond me. And I bet they do not like this weather, if they are truly Spanish.'

'Hah! Then do you like the cold less than the Spaniards, being from Africa or wherever?' she questioned.

'Addy,' he reminded her, 'I am a Londoner, same as you. More than you in fact, as Mother Hopkins said she found you in Liverpool and you spoke no English till you were three!'

'I have heard those tales!' she retaliated. 'She said *you* were bought for threepence from a blackamoor maid in Newgate.'

'And you were found on the Mersey foreshore sucking fish eyes out of the heads the fishwives had thrown away, talking only in Dutch or Welsh or other gibberish.'

Addy made a huffy sound and they walked as far as Leicester Fields in silence. Sheep huddled together in the centre of the square for warmth and the poor girl watching them stamped her feet against the frozen earth. The usual stallholders had vanished, and the gangs of builders worked slower than normal, the wooden scaffolding around so many new buildings frosted like man-made spiders' webs against the city sky.

'Town is so quiet, Cato!' Addy moaned. 'Everyone is at the fair except us.'

Cato was beginning to agree. Some of the shops had their windows shuttered and closed as if it was Christmas morning, and even the beggars and crossing sweepers seemed to have vanished. Apart from the crowd of ragged children around the door of a bakers – for the warmth, Cato thought – there was scarce half the number of people on the street as usual.

He pulled Addy along with him. 'Come on, we have work to do. We are sent to St James's!'

'Oh, Cato, look around you! Any mark worth his salt will be rugged up by as big a fire as can be safely made, or –' she smiled a wicked smile – 'they will be out on the ice at the fair watching the Russian bear dance! And just think of the quids there'll be there, wanting to be spent, calling to us to be set free from those rich men's pockets. Please, Cato? It will be more fun with two and I have my cards.' She hugged his arm.

Cato stopped. They had reached St James's Square and it was quiet here too. The houses were so big – huge and sleepy and just-built new. All were painted a deep rich cream, and the imposing front doors were a shiny beetle black. The light in the windows seemed to glow golden. Cato sighed, and for an instant imagined some kind of life that involved a home in a place like this.

'Can you manage those keyholes, Cato?' Addy asked, and his dream faded. He pulled himself back into the present. He could see that most of the front doors had the newest style locks, the ones that required keys with changeable bits.

'I'll have to see if I can take a look at one before it's set in a door. Take one apart a couple of times. But anyway, folks are always forgetting they have back doors and side doors.'

'And windows!'

'Oh, I know our mark's here somewhere,' Cato said, looking around.

Addy stamped her feet to keep warm. 'Can we go to the fair now, Cato. Please?'

'There's so much money in this half a mile, but in St Giles, scarce a breath away, they're fighting over a farthing in the gutter. Life's not fair, Addy.'

'No one ever said it was.'

'We shall have to make it fairer then.' Cato took a deep breath. 'You can almost smell the cash round here.'

'Cato, that smell is only the roast chestnut man, and there'll be a deal more chestnuts and hot pies and hot everything down at the fair!' Addy looked at him with her best puppy eyes. 'Come on, Cato?'

Cato sighed. She was right. 'The fair then,' he said.

As they turned away, a carriage pulled by two fine matched bays drew in ahead. The footman jumped down and opened a door, and a young woman wearing a floor-length velvet cloak, edged with white fur, lowered a satin-shod foot on to the pavement.

She was a picture of such radiance and beauty that Addy stopped in her tracks and stared. Cato had to nudge her to make her stop.

'Quit staring, Add!'

The woman stared back for a second. Her face was powdered white as the fur that framed it, and her lips were painted deep red. Cato shuddered and pulled Addy away.

'Hey! I was only looking!' Addy protested. 'I never seen so much rabbit except in Smithfield!

She must have more slosh than is proper in a get-up like that. Maybe that's our mark, Cato.'

Cato turned back and saw a man getting out of the carriage to follow the woman into a grand house. He felt a chill run down his spine that wasn't caused by the air or the frost underfoot.

'Now *you're* staring,' said Addy. 'Do you think they might be possibles? State of that cloak! We'd get five guineas for it at least, I reckon!'

'I've seen her face before, I know it,' Cato said as they walked back through Leicester Fields.

'Friend of yours then?' Addy smiled. 'From Turnmill Street? I don't think I seen her round Clerkenwell or up the Garden.'

'Don't be daft, Addy. I can't recall where I've seen her.'

'Ooh, you've gone all serious. Did you really know her? So who is she then?' Addy pestered.

'I'm trying to remember. Some gentry,' replied Cato, racking his brain for a reminder.

Addy snorted. 'Well, I think I could have told you that!'

'No, Addy – could be London, could be some country lady. I've been in and out of that many families over the years. The number of times I've been some nob's slave I've lost count of the names. But I know her, I'm sure.'

'Well, remember quick.' Addy pulled out her cards. 'I shall have to warm my hands up good and proper first, then we'll turn round enough rhino for supper and more besides.'

The Thames was transformed. Instead of the muddy brown river there was now a huge field of white stretching across to Southwark, dotted with tents and booths and stalls like a tented city magicked into existence overnight. Curls of smoke from a hundred little fires wisped up into the air like grey velvet ribbons.

'Why don't the fires melt holes?' Addy said as they reached what had been the river bank.

'It's too thick, and too cold. I expect more water just freezes every night,' Cato said, almost slipping on the steps down to the ice. He had to speak almost into her ear because of the noise: scratchy fiddles and droning pipes, shouts for hog roasts, nuts and potatoes, calls to see a 'real unicorn' and a 'true-life mermaid' and a woman who 'gives birth to live rabbits before your very eyes!'

'So you'll set me off and watch my back?' Addy asked.

'Don't I always?' said Cato.

After they'd looked at the Russian bear and the unicorn – both too sad to contemplate for long, Cato thought – Addy found a half-barrel abandoned near the booths and turned it over, dusted it off and laid out her cards. Cato watched at a distance, pretending he was part of the crowd waiting to see the woman give birth to rabbits.

Addy looked small and slightly untidy, her light brown hair falling on either side of her face to her shoulders. Her features were sharp, her mouth smiled more than frowned, and Cato thought that most people wouldn't look twice if she ran past as they crossed the Strand or Covent Garden. Addy was small for twelve, a melt-into-the-crowd sort of grey-eyed girl. But when she started up her patter, with a voice loud enough to crack stone, she came alive.

'Laydies, gennelmen!' Addy shuffled the cards so fast they rapped a kind of tattoo on the barrel top. 'Give me your time, your concentration, your full and undivided attention, and see if you can earn yourselves some pennies! I won't ask once –' she threw the cards from one hand to the other in a perfect arc and one or two punters slowed to watch – 'I won't ask twice!' The cards flew back into the other hand. 'You find the lady, find our Good Queen Anne, Lord love her, and you can beat me.' She fanned the cards in her hand and made the queen seem to rise out of the pack by itself. 'There she is! Oops, most sorry, Your Majesty!' She turned the picture card over face down on the barrel with a slap.

'And there's her subjects, the two of spades and the nine of cups! Watch 'em, watch 'em, laydies and gennelmen, young and old. Watch her now an' see where she goes.'

There were one or two watching closely as Addy slid the cards around one another.

'Have a free go, sir! Yes, you!' She pointed at a printer's apprentice, black hands folded over his blacker apron. 'Can you tell? Can you?' she asked.

The apprentice shrugged and pointed an inky finger at the middle card and Addy turned it over and affected surprise.

'Oh, sir! Most intelligent young man!' she cooed.

'Don't give me that!' the apprentice snarled. 'I seen this game done before! As soon as I puts my money down, you'll have magicked that queen away.'

'Now, young master,' Addy said, smiling at him, 'would I do such a thing? A maid like myself?'

Cato heard his cue and made his way out of the crowd, penny in hand. He pushed the apprentice aside and stood opposite Addy.

'Here's my cash says I can find your lady, miss.' The apprentice looked at Cato sideways and Cato smiled back.

Addy's cards slid almost faster than the eye across the barrel top and Cato took his time following and picking out the queen, even asking the apprentice his opinion, then with much deliberation and effort chose his card. Addy flexed her fingers, bit her lip and turned the card. When they saw the queen's face, the little crowd that had gathered to watch raised quite a cheer. Addy made a show of world weariness and Cato winked at the apprentice and moved out of the way so a man with a red nose who stank of gin could take his place.

Cato stood at a distance for a while until he was sure that Addy had enough punters, and that no one was giving her any trouble, then he took his money to the chestnut man.

He was on his way back when he passed the rabbit-birthing tent for the third time and bothered to read the sign.

LIVE RABBITS BORN FROM A FAIR KENTISH MAID! it said in foot-high black letters. There was a picture too, of a bonneted girl with red cheeks. And underneath: NO ARTIFICE. NO DEVILRY! A MOST NATURAL WONDER! VERILY A SECOND MARIAH HOPKINS!

Cato almost dropped the chestnuts. Mariah was Mother Hopkins's given Christian name.

He caught the bag of nuts before they hit the ground, but then he heard Addy's voice, clear and sharp as a knife, calling 'Ca-to!' and he ran through the crowd and pulled her away from four seriously cross-looking apprentices.

'Addy, you'll never guess – there was a live rabbits booth with Mother's name on it—'

'Hold your breath for running, Cato. I can still hear the 'prentices!'

They ran in between the stalls and booths back to the Strand Steps, the wooden soles of the apprentices clattering close behind.

'Faster, Cato!' Addy shouted.

The gang of inky-aproned apprentices were shouting and throwing things at them as they skidded straight into the Russian bear's handler, a tall blond youth who swore loudly in authentic Russian as he hit the floor. Luckily he swore even more when the pack of apprentices careered round the corner, slid on the ice and fell on top of him in a heap.

Cato pulled Addy up behind him on to the river bank and they legged it as far as Portugal Street before stopping to catch their breath.

'I've told you, Addy, steer clear of the 'prentices. They always come back at you mob-handed!'

'We got away, didn't we?' she puffed. 'Anyway, you should have rescued me sooner! What was you going on about? Live rabbits! It's a scam old as the hills an' you should know it.'

'You never saw the bill stuck outside in big huge letters. Isn't her first name Mariah?'

'Who are you on about? The cat's mother?' Addy asked, getting more and more confused.

'No, Addy, our Mother Hopkins. She's Mariah.'

Addy nodded, but she wasn't really listening: she was too busy counting up her pennies.

'Two shillings! Well, near enough. Ooh, I'm good!'

'And didn't she say as she'd done work with the fairs?' Cato continued. 'When she ran away from the big house where she worked? She was a maid, she said. Remember?'

'What?'

'Mother Hopkins! When she travelled with the fair, she did a turn, giving birth to live rabbits!'

'Wouldn't half mind seeing that!' Addy laughed. 'Dare you to ask her how she done it!'

Cato was quiet. Mother Hopkins wasn't one for talking about the past. She'd go on about jobs they'd done, but her past, before Arabella, was like a closed book.

Addy tied her money up in her purse. 'You know what Ma's like: "Don't go looking under stones – something'll come up and bite you!" That's what she always says. Bet you don't ask her!'

Cato walked on. Addeline was right. 'Anyway, Mother'll be the one doing the asking, I reckon. Asking us whether we saw anything up St James's,' he said.

'Ah. Yes. She'll be pleased to hear my pocket. But you're right as usual, Cato. If she thinks we've been at the fair all afternoon . . . What about that woman, that lady? Her with the cloak to the ground and the fancy slippers. And you thought you knew her face, remember? She looked the business.'

Cato held out the bag of still warm chestnuts. 'S'pose so,' he said.

'See, we're in the best of all possible situations: quids, a sprinkling of information and some warm chestnuts! We'll be set for the best place by the fire, I warrant!'

4. A Fine Pair of Pigeons

IT WAS the next morning when Cato remembered. He was trying to fit back together the newest of the barrel locks just made in Staffordshire, sent over by Daley the locksmith's boy. Mother Hopkins made sure the locksmith at the Aldwych always had a bottle of something extra so that Cato could be up to date with his practice. The pieces lay strewn about on the seat of a stool. It was like the hardest kind of puzzle, seeing which tiny piece of brass fitted where, and although it was vexing, it was worth it just for the feeling of achievement he had when he'd mastered a lock. The harder he stared and thought, the more he seemed to be almost thinking about nothing – nothing but the actual lock in front of him. It was as if he had to approach the lock sideways, like a shy child, not letting it realize it was the object of his attention. It was during one of these reveries that the name of the woman he'd seen in St James's came flying into his head.

'Elizabeth Walker!' he said, not looking up.

'Is that the name of your new sweetheart?' Bella was standing by the window, holding a looking glass and trying to blacken her eyebrows with a bit of charcoal she had pulled out of the fire.

'No! And you look as if two black caterpillars are making a meeting on your forehead,' Cato said.

Bella stuck out her tongue but looked at herself again and began rubbing some of the charcoal off.

'Elizabeth Walker.' Cato picked up a tiny brass screw and held it up to the light. 'You don't remember? She was the daughter of those nobs in Greenwich. Where Sam worked.'

'Now that *was* a nice house. At least from the outside. Maybe we can get one like that in Bath,' Bella suggested.

'I think she lives in an even finer one now,' replied Cato. 'Unless, that is, she was only visiting.'

'Was it the woman you saw in the velvet? The one Addy was prattling on about?'

Suddenly the door opened and the cold wind that blew in scattered some of the lighter metalwork off the stool and on to the floor. Cato jumped up.

'God's teeth!' he said, crawling across the floor after them.

Bella laughed. 'You swear like an old man!'

Addy and Mother Hopkins came in, stamping to rid themselves of the cold.

'Watch my lock!' Cato wailed, but Addy made a beeline for the fire and her feet knocked the brass screws, and fixings rolled farther away.

Cato crawled after them. 'It will take me all day to find the pieces now and that lock was five shillings' worth!' he moaned.

'I promise I'll help as soon as my fingers are thawed out,' Addy said, hands outstretched in front of the flames.

'And didn't Old Man Daley give you the lock for nothing?' Mother Hopkins asked, placing her copious black bag on the table with a thud.

'Yes, but if I don't return it, we'll be paying.' Cato took a red cotton handkerchief from his back pocket and began collecting up the parts and tying them inside.

'*You'll* be paying,' Bella said, pinching at her cheeks to redden them. 'I'm off to the White Raven. To pour coffee for gentlemen who are, sadly, gentlemen in name only.'

'Hah! Then they will appreciate you, being as you are a maid in name only,' said Cato.

Addy laughed and Bella cuffed him across the side of the head on her way out.

'You provoke each other too much,' Mother Hopkins said, sitting in her chair and warming herself. 'There are enough people in this world who will provoke you without you and Bella making it a family sport. She is your sister. You should remember that and treat her so.'

Cato was about to say that very many people treated their flesh-and-blood sisters a good deal worse. He had seen Daley the locksmith's boy and his sister come to such blows in the street that they pulled whole handfuls of one another's hair clean out. But he shut his mouth again. He wondered if he had any blood sisters, any real sisters. Girls with hair as black and woolly as his own and skin as dark as the tabletop. He sighed and shook the thought away.

Addy had collected some pieces of lock and handed them over, smiling. Her hair was coming undone from where she had tied it up and it fell around her face.

'I remembered the name. Of the woman we saw,' he said.

'Oh?' Mother Hopkins looked up.

'I've seen her before, only younger, and then her face was rounder and her hair wasn't hidden inside that hood . . .'

'Oh, that velvet cape was so lush!' Addy said.

'Cut to the chase, Cato!' snapped Mother Hopkins.

'She was that Elizabeth Walker, Captain Walker's daughter. Of Greenwich,' Cato said.

Mother Hopkins looked interested and leaned forward. 'I did read of her wedding in the *London Gazette*. She married John Stapleton, the *honourable* Sir John Stapleton, who is already wealthier than all the nabobs of India caught up together in one room. And as soon as his father, the Marquess of Byfield, dies – and the marquess is not long for this world, so I've heard – he will have as much gold as the Bank of England. Sir John Stapleton is a Member of Parliament, a post his father paid handsomely for. Well, that is what's said.' Mother took her clay pipe from its place at the side of her chair and tapped it twice to empty out the old tobacco.

'So she married him, did she?' Cato said. 'That Stapleton, that lump of a boy who came calling – I told you about him – he gave her some diamonds. Great rocks like boiled sugar. I never seen the like since. That dullard a Member of Parliament!' He shook his head. 'Wonders never cease.'

'No, my boy,' Mother Hopkins said, and smiled. 'They certainly do not.'

That evening Mother called her family to a meeting. She sat in her chair nearest to the fire as everyone piled in around her. Jack and Sam remained standing, looking flash in their chairman's livery – long brocade coats and matching hats. Bella sat at the table pouring coffee and Addy and Cato were shelling walnuts as fast as they were being eaten.

'Bella tells me your mark has found you.' Jack stood with his back to the fireplace, his hands lifting the tails of his fancy jacket out of the way of the heat.

'So it seems,' Mother Hopkins said.

'Sam and me thought you might try the Careys of Mayfair. They have plenty of money and the eldest son, Alexander, is so free with the rhino it practically falls from his britches as he walks – which of course he never does. You'll have seen him in Hyde Park driving the best matched pair of Arabians I've seen in town! He's ripe, Mother!'

'Pah! The Careys!' Mother spat into the fire.

'Or Lord Fitzadam,' Jack continued. 'That man is so old he is practically waiting to fall into his own grave! And he has no heirs. His money is waiting to be plucked from him before some other rogue does it first.'

Mother Hopkins sat up. 'Old Fitz never wronged anyone his whole life! You know my ways by now, Jack, and I am not to be tainted with honest money! Never! The man may be old but that does not make him a gull in my book. Old age comes to us all, and although I am sure you can't believe that now, you will one day.'

Cato said nothing but he smiled. It was always better to take money from those that deserved it. Poor Edgar and his broken heart still weighed heavy on his mind and had caused him to wake in the night more than once. What if a girl treated *him* like that? What if he gave his heart to someone like Bella, who would throw it back in his face while she smiled?

Jack folded his arms and sighed. 'I know you might not pay heed, but me and Sam are of the same mind on this,' he said, shifting his weight.

'And what mind is that?' Mother Hopkins asked, her voice clipped.

'We don't like it, Ma, and that's the truth. Sam especially so.' Jack took a deep breath and looked at Sam for reassurance before he went on. 'He says just the thought of having anything to do with those people makes his blood chill.'

Mother Hopkins shifted in her chair. 'It is, ooh, four, five years past since he worked in their household,' she said. 'For a woman like Elizabeth – unless she has changed character – that might as well be a lifetime. And remember, Jack, to those people servants all have but one face, and that counts as double if their skin is not white.'

'Mother's right, Jack,' Cato said. 'The number of times I am asked if I am so and so's brother or if I might know a great acquaintance of theirs who just happens to have the same colour skin as me, you would not believe it.'

'You forget I work with Sam. I know all that!' Jack reminded them. 'But Sam is well known about town and he wants no more attention drawn to himself than is possible.'

Mother Hopkins sat back. 'Our Sam can speak for himself,' she said, looking straight at him.

Sam shifted and accepted a cup of coffee from Bella. He took a sip before answering. 'I am sorry, Mother. I know what you have done for me. All of you.' He looked from Addy, to Bella and finally to Cato. 'I know your bravery. And I am ashamed to admit I am scared of these people. Captain Walker is not a man to be trifled with! And they remind me that I have a mother, a real mother – begging your pardon, Mother Hopkins – who I am powerless to help.' He looked away and Jack rested his hand on his friend's shoulder.

Mother Hopkins blew out a cloud of blue smoke before she spoke. 'So be it. You can stay in the background – but you'll do any shifting though, any transport we might need, and you'll be our eyes and ears on the street.'

Sam nodded.

'We will,' said Jack. 'And we'll come to Bath. We've talked it through, and since the Queen is so in love with the place, there's more nobs than ever taking the waters. We reckon we could clean up. Big fish in a small pond, me and Sam. So we'll help. But with our heads down on this one, Mother. And you must all tread so carefully. And remember –' he nodded at Cato – 'you'll not forget you're known to that woman too.'

'Miss Walker never looked at me for more than half an instant!' Cato said. He was thinking that as Jack and Sam were backing out, there'd be a chance for him to take a lead in planning and make a role for himself that didn't involve being sold or bought or waiting on others.

'So you have made your decision already then – it's to be the Stapletons?' asked Sam.

Mother Hopkins nodded. 'One more thing, chickens,' she said. 'Not a word more to Ez and Sally in the bar. They know better than to ask questions, and you all should know just as well to keep your mouths shut and your tongues still. This is not their business and I would not have them without work when we leave.'

'Of course not, Ma,' Jack said, and the others agreed. 'And we're off to the Garden to work!'

'You will be careful, won't you, Mother?' Sam asked before he followed Jack out.

Mother Hopkins smiled at him, her face rosy in the glow of the fire. 'Oh, we'll be more than careful, Sam, you know me. I never intend setting foot in Newgate or any other place like it as long as I live and breathe.'

5. The Web Begun

IN THE front bar of The Vipers, Ezra Spinoza poured the ale into Jack's own pewter tankard. Jack nodded his thanks and turned to Cato.

'If that bloody Ivanski gets any nearer to my Bella, I'll knock his block off and send it back to Russia in a box!' He slumped forward on the polished wooden bar of The Vipers next to Cato. 'Bella is mine and no one seems to have told him. Go on, ask anyone, ask 'em! I'm her true love and everyone knows it!' He downed his ale. 'I've loved her ever since I was younger than you and with no home of my own. Before Mother took me in! Before I knew how to love, I loved her!' Jack's grey eyes clouded over. 'Bella kissed me, told me I was the one for her – we were barely fourteen but I knew she was my . . . my destiny.'

Cato couldn't help laughing. 'That is ale talking, Jack!' he said. 'She is Arabella Hopkins! And I know she is soft on you, but how many times has she been married off to others?'

'That was just work!' Jack protested. 'She'll be wed to me as soon as I can scrape enough cash together.'

'Then don't look at her now, Jack!'

'I can't help it. It's like one of them itches you have to scratch. I know she's there, I know she's smilin' at him an' battin' her lashes at him, doing the cow eyes just the way she does for me.'

'Come on, Jack. Come upstairs and forget her. Ez'll keep an eye on them, won't you?'

The big man nodded.

Jack sighed. 'I wish it were that easy. Love, Cato, is a bad mistress.' He looked once more at Bella simpering at the young man and Cato couldn't help but look too.

'You know she has to get the accent right,' Cato said. 'And Mother Hopkins couldn't find any other Russians in a hurry. I suggested it – he keeps that poor bear in a stable over Southwark.'

'I bet I could have found an uglier one down in Deptford,' moaned Jack. 'A real ugly swine with no teeth and tattoos the colour of oranges going mouldy up his arms. I mean, look at your man there!'

Cato looked. The Russian was taller than Jack, and although no better looking – the Russian was fairer with clear blue eyes – he was obviously well off. He was dressed in a fine sheepskin jacket and good leather boots. And it was obvious, even to Cato, that Bella was enjoying her work a little too much.

There was a sudden blast of cold air from the street outside and Addy stood in the doorway carrying a bundle of clothes and wearing the tallest, whitest fur hat Cato had ever seen.

'Come on, yer leery kinchen, give us a hand or two with these duds!' she said.

Cato and Jack looked at each other.

'Addy, you sound more like the thimble twister you are every day!' Jack shouted across The Vipers, and most of the regulars laughed.

Cato went across and took some of the clothes. 'You should watch what you say in public,' he whispered.

'They all know us here, Cato. We're coney catchers, and the best around. And what's more we've the salad here to catch those rabbits.'

'Hah! The Stapletons are rather more than rabbits, Addy.'

'But rabbits all the same, and this hat is the very thing in St Petersburg. Oi! Ivan,' Addy said as she walked in front of Bella and the Russian.

'This good hat, yes? This bene shappo, Ivanski?' Addy plonked it on to Bella's head.

The Russian smiled. 'Da. Is good, yes. Da. Bella real Cossack devotchka.'

'There. One happy customer,' said Addy.

Bella smiled, but her words were cold. 'Hold your tongue, Addy, and go away.'

Addy pulled a face, turned on her heel and strode away. 'Why does Bella get all the good jobs?' she said to Cato as they went upstairs. 'Have you seen the state of these threads? Serious splash-up stuff.' She held up a jacket edged with fur. 'If this is the Russian style, I could see me in St Petersburg, sailing into town in one of these!'

'I thought you hated girls' clothes,' said Cato.

Addy shrugged. 'This is different. I wouldn't mind being a Russian girl. Just look at these boots!'

Mother Hopkins was sitting at the table writing a letter, pen in one hand, pipe in the other.

'Addeline, good, you've the clothes. And Cato. I must talk to you both.'

She signed the letter and blotted it. Cato read the address on the envelope: it was to the Stapleton house but it was addressed to the housekeeper. Someone would be working inside – he was sure of it.

Mother Hopkins looked up. 'Bella will be going to a party on Friday night as the Russian.'

Cato looked at Addy. He hadn't expected things to be moving this quickly, and from the look on her face, neither had she.

'This Friday? Only three days away? That's a bit quick,' Addy said as she warmed herself by the fire.

'I'm not sure how good her accent will be by then, Mother,' Cato warned.

'Bella knows. She'll have to nail it down or keep her mouth shut. Either way, there's a party in Mayfair and we need her there. The Stapletons will be attending and we can't afford to miss it. She's to be Ekaterina, Countess of . . . of . . .'

'Of St Petersburg?' Addy suggested.

'No! Too obvious.' Mother Hopkins folded the letter and reached for the stick of red sealing wax, holding it in the candle flame till it softened. 'Cato? Any ideas? Did you not fetch an atlas from the bookseller's?'

Cato was opening the bundle of clothes. There were the dresses for Bella in the Russian style, edged with fur and heavy with gold thread, and a smaller bundle of servants' clothes . . . girls' clothes – the stays looked too small for Bella.

'An atlas!' Cato had passed the morning in the bookseller's in St Paul's Churchyard. He'd spent hours poring over engravings of men with heads in their chests and women with tails like fish instead of legs. There were some truly excellent 'Dying Words' ballads, one by a pirate who'd sailed out of Port Royal, another by Claude Duvall, the gentleman highwayman, and he'd read a whole volume of poems by an author he'd never heard of before being thrown out for reading the goods and not buying. But he'd managed to forget the atlas.

Mother Hopkins dolloped the melted wax on the edge of the letter. 'Addeline, the Salters' seal please.'

Addy scrabbled in the dresser drawer amongst a variety of the best (and worst) London families' seals, stolen or recreated over the years.

Cato tried to remember the maps. He'd looked at one or two but they weren't half as interesting as the prints of giants who dwell in the deserts of Africa.

'Maybe I could talk to the Russian downstairs, get an idea of the country and the principal towns from him?' Cato suggested.

'You didn't look, did you, Cato?' Addy said smugly. 'I'll bet he was head down in some ballad mongers reading cod poetry!'

Mother Hopkins pressed the seal hard into the melted wax. 'This is a most important enterprise, Cato,' she said. 'I would have thought you understood that.'

'Honestly, Mother, I do.' Cato felt himself flush.

'Even though your part in this lay will be behind the scenes, you have to know that Bella's deception must be entirely plausible.' Mother Hopkins sucked hard on her pipe. 'Addeline, run down and tell Bella to question her Russian on his home town.'

Addy was about to go when she saw the stays and servants' clothes. 'Who are they for?' She curled her lip as she picked out the dark flannel stays and skirts.

'Well, we need someone inside the Stapletons' household.' Mother Hopkins didn't look up.

Cato and Addy looked at each other. Cato couldn't imagine Addy in that get-up.

'Can't he go?' Addy pointed at Cato.

'They might rumble him,' said Mother. 'It's too much of a risk. And he's playing fiddle at the party on Friday – it's an African orchestra, the latest fashion apparently.' She smiled.

Cato tried not to look anxious; he had neglected his playing since Bella's 'wedding'.

'Will we rehearse, Mother?' he asked. 'What if I can't—?'

'There's never any *can't*, Cato. If you don't know the tunes, play along quietly and smile.'

Addy folded her arms. 'He gets to play music while I sweep up ashes! I'll not do it. A housemaid!'

'Cato.' Mother Hopkins ignored Addy and handed Cato the envelope. 'Here is the letter for the Stapletons recommending Addeline Hammond as maid of all work. Listen well, Addy, for Hammond is your name until our lay is done. According to this, you have worked for the Salters of Highgate for these two summers past.' Addy made to speak but Mother Hopkins shushed her. 'Sam has sweet-talked the Stapletons' current kitchen maid and has already promised her a better position with Mendes in Cheapside. And, Sam told me not an hour since, she has packed her things already. We must be sure it is Addeline who fills the post, so, Cato, give the letter to Jack and Sam to take to St James's tonight. Quick now, before dark! And, Addy, get yourself down to The Vipers to sound out the Russian.'

Mother Hopkins looked from one to the other. 'I'll have no dissent, chickens. We depend on each other utterly! And if you don't know that by now . . .'

That Friday found Addeline squirming and uncomfortable in her new woollen maid's uniform. Cato walked alongside her – he'd promised to go with her as far as Leicester Fields. It was a done deal: Addy was to start as the Stapletons' kitchen maid at noon and she could no more wriggle out of the job than she could wriggle out of her newly laced stays.

'Stays!' she spat. 'They are the devil's own work!'

Cato couldn't keep a straight face.

'And you –' she poked him hard under the ribs – 'can stop with your smug face! I hope the strings of your fiddle cause your fingers one quarter of the pain I am in on account of this infernal corsetry.'

'You must not fidget so, Addy, or your new employers will assume you are ridden with fleas,' Cato teased her.

'I would rather be home to a thousand, thousand fleas than wear these hateful instruments of torture all day,' Addy protested.

'You will soon be used to them. Think of the number of times I had to wear one of those damnable metal collars. And once – somewhere uncivilized up north, it was – they chained me up in their kitchen like a dog! All you have to do is wear what other women manage without complaint. I have only ever heard Bella ask for her stays to be laced tighter!'

'What do you know of women? What you read in your poems? And Bella doesn't have to fetch and carry and scrub and clean. And she gets the fancy threads and a purse stuffed so full of fake rhino she can hardly carry it!'

'True.' Cato nodded. 'Bella always gets the good parts.'

'What I wouldn't give to be a duchess!' Addy sighed.

'Bella's not a duchess, she's a countess, from Pskoff,' Cato said.

'The town that sounds like a fart! I hope her Ivan didn't make the place up out of air.'

'I looked it up. It does exist. And she's to play a wealthy young widow,' Cato added.

'*I* could be wealthy,' said Addy.

'You wouldn't carry the clothes. You'd twitch and complain about the weight of silks and you'd never sit long enough for the quality.'

Addeline humphed.

'I must go, Addy. Mother says you are to St James's straightway and no stopping. I have one hundred new dance tunes to practise before tonight. What if these musicians are no better than me and I have to carry the tune? It doesn't bear thinking on!'

Addeline's face was still a mask of sulkiness.

'Your things.' Cato held out the bundle he had carried for her. 'And smile! You make the sourest housemaid in London.'

Addy smiled a fixed smile back at him.

'Your cards are in there,' said Cato. 'I hid them – they're wrapped in that ballad I bought for you. The one about the pirate; you liked that.'

'That was different, that was a story. And thank you, Cato, for the cards. I am grateful for these old friends.'

'Keep them hidden!' Cato warned her. 'Mother will flay us both if they're discovered.'

Addeline smiled properly and took the bundle. For a moment he thought she would hug him, but she just sighed. 'I hope this damnable lay is over quick,' she said.

'You will be a most excellent maid, Addy. I know it.'

Addy held out her skirts. 'Sometimes I am sure I would have preferred to be a boy.'

'You make a fine girl, Addy,' Cato said, and turned away so she would not see him blushing. 'Take care. Keep your eyes and ears open.'

'I'll miss you, Cato!' she called.

Cato watched until she'd turned the corner. Three weeks. He couldn't remember a time when they'd been apart for so long.

6. A Merry Dance

'MUSICIANS! MUSICIANS attend here at once!' The large man with rather tightly cut breeches and new wig waved a silk handkerchief above his head. Cato was standing in the ballroom of a fine house in Hanover Square in the West End. Armies of servants were busy pinning up garlands of ivy and rosemary on the walls and sweeping the polished wooden floor. There were mirrors as big as the walls at The Vipers, and a thousand candles and their reflections fluttered and danced all around.

'Attention please!' The man clapped his hands together. 'I am Master Cowell, responsible for the auditory entertainment this evening, and it is down to my contrivance that you have been selected . . .' He paused and looked around. Cato followed his gaze. The other musicians were two elderly African men with grey beards and only enough teeth between them to suck gruel; a young lad with a kind face and the most elaborate silver collar Cato had seen for some time; a fair-skinned Negro, almost yellow, holding a bass viol; and a tall and haughty dark-skinned young man with patterns of spirals in tiny raised scars on his cheeks. Not the pox – Cato could see that these were deliberate whorls snaking over his cheekbones.

Master Cowell pointed at them in turn, counting.

'There are only six? I asked for eight! Eight, I said. Where are my drummers? The Gold Coast Gordons?' He looked at the youth with the scars. 'Do you know of them? I was told they were the best African-styled drummers in London.'

The young man smiled and spoke. He had the most elegant voice Cato had ever heard. Indeed, if his eyes had been closed, he would have said he was listening to a gentleman, and one with money.

'They are not known to me, sir. And I can honestly say that the name is about as African as a Yorkshire pudding.'

The greybeards sniggered.

'Good, good,' Master Cowell said, obviously not listening. 'And, you two!' He pointed at the greybeards. 'For God's own sakes look to your mouths and keep them shut! Your few teeth shame both yourselves and our orchestra.'

The scarred youth raised one eyebrow. 'This is unlike any orchestra I have ever seen in my life, sir.'

Master Cowell laughed. 'You are just a black! What know you of orchestras? This is a completely novel experiment. The African Orchestra! Utterly of my own devising!'

'I am much more than just a black, sir! I am Prince Quarmy of Bonny. It is only your ignorance that cannot see that. In my father's court we have the best musicians from the Bight of Benin to the Bight of Bonny. The Asante court musicians are legendary!'

One of the old men tugged at the youth's sleeve and whispered: 'Careful with your words, young man. Prince or not, you'll get us all put out on the street without even the sweet sound of a few coins rattling in our pockets.'

Master Cowell stared. 'Listen, boy. I do not care if you are the Holy Roman Emperor! Tonight you are my orchestra and you will play your damnedest or you shall not see my money.' He clapped his hands again. 'You must dress yourselves in the costumes you will find downstairs, quick sharp! Then up here to strike up an African sarabande – it is my own composition. Costumes now!' The music master ushered them downstairs to a room next to the kitchens.

'They expect us to wear this?' Quarmy held up a scrap of what looked like black and white ponyskin, and from the curl of his lip Cato imagined he had at least served princes if he was not one himself. 'We will freeze! Outside snow lies in the streets and we are expected to wear nothing! This is so much foolishness!'

Cato had to stop himself laughing, but his mood changed when he saw one of the old men's backs, a mass of weals from a whipping long ago.

'You reading my back, young man?' he said when he saw Cato looking. 'The Good Fortune Estate, east out of Spanish Town, Jamaica, fifteen years ago, I reckon.'

The others all looked too. 'I tried to stop the buckra – overseer to you – selling my baby boy far away. I didn't sleep on my back for near enough three months.'

The youth with the collar took off his shirt and turned round. 'I got mine in Richmond just one month past. I can no more play any tune than fly.' He lowered his voice. 'My name is Rowlands. I'm off into London as soon as I can loose this collar round my neck and slip away into the city.'

The old men nodded but Quarmy looked at Rowlands as if he was a speck of dirt.

Rowlands bridled, and Cato worried that he'd knock the Prince of Bonny down in an instant.

Cato leaned close. 'I can help you with that collar. If you let me, I can spring the lock in two seconds. I've been able to pick those collars since I could walk!'

Rowlands nodded, his face flushed with relief.

Quarmy dropped the pony-skin back on to the floor. 'Well, I for one am not having it. These costumes are an affront!'

Suddenly two white men – one short and dark-haired, the other tall and fiercely red-headed – came and stood in the kitchen doorway, watching them change.

'This is no sideshow, gentlemen.' Quarmy moved to shut the door. 'And tell Master Cowell we will not humiliate ourselves in these scraps!'

'No, um . . .' one said.

'Too right,' said the other, holding out a hand. 'We're the Gordons. Balls, masques and revels.'

'Drumming and percussion.' The short one held up a hand drum. 'The latest African styles. Of the highest quality. We've played for the crowned heads of Europe.'

'Well, some of them,' said the tall one.

'There's none better!'

The room went quiet.

The tall redhead looked sheepish. 'Even if we're not actually blood brothers. Or, as you may have noticed, Africans.'

The smaller one lifted up a scrap of pony-skin. 'And we are most definitely in agreement with you about the outfits!'

The oldest greybeard burst out laughing.

While the drummers introduced themselves, Cato took a small pick out of his waistcoat pocket, leaned over to Rowlands and slipped the lock in two seconds.

'My God! 'Tis done.' Rowlands smiled and hid the collar deep under the pile of pony-skins. 'As if the metal was butter!'

'Anything is easy,' Cato said, 'if you know how to do it.'

When Master Cowell returned to chivvy them up to the ballroom, he was furious. 'You are an African orchestra! I am spending good money on authentic African musicians.'

The Gordons moved to leave but Master Cowell was so desperate he shut the door. 'Oh, you'll all stay. But you would look so much more authentic in the skins!' He shook his head. 'From what I have heard, these blacks are all as strong as oxes and a bit of cold wouldn't hurt!'

Quarmy stepped forward. His voice was low and soft but so full of authority that any trace of doubt Cato might have had about his heritage was wiped away. 'We will not wear them. If you want music, we will play in our own clothes, like gentlemen.'

There was a chorus of ayes and Cowell held Quarmy's gaze for a few seconds, but it was the music master who looked away first.

Up in the ballroom, the servants had left except for one small girl polishing up an enormous looking glass. Her face was red with effort and Cato thought of Addy in the fine house in St James's. Maybe she would see the Stapletons as they left for the ball. Maybe she would be readying Lady Elizabeth. He took out his violin.

More likely Addy would be in the kitchen washing the pots.

The music on the stands was clear enough – a sarabande – but made dull in the writing. Quarmy suggested a minuet instead and started up a strong tune, the one Cato had heard last in the pleasure gardens south of the river and a favourite of Bella's.

Rowlands looked uncomfortable. 'It's not the collar now, Cato; it's the fact that I am no musician. I should slip away before the dancing,' he said.

'Don't be a fool, man. You are a slave and have a duty to your owner,' Quarmy said.

Rowlands smarted. 'You are the fool!'

The greybeards held Rowlands back and scowled at Quarmy. 'You have no idea, young man, none at all.'

Cato tried to keep the peace. 'Come now, brothers, we are to work.' He made Rowlands sit close by him. 'Just follow our movements, and smile,' he said. 'I'll cover for you.'

Rowlands still looked nervous. 'Then truly I owe you my soul, sir.'

Cato had forgotten how much he enjoyed playing. The Gordons were excellent drummers, and Quarmy and the light-skinned boy, Isaac, were good. The well-dressed crowd filled the ballroom and the dancing began. After Master Cowell's dirge-like sarabande they played two of the most popular minuets and then there was a lull in the dancing. Cato scanned the crowd for Bella. So many colours, silk and satin, and embroidery that must have vexed the eyes of roomfuls of needlemen and -women in garrets all over Spitalfields. Women wearing rubies redder than a glass of claret, gentlemen with powdered wigs and buckles on their shoes that would fetch good money if you knew where to take them. A woman wearing black pearls and green emeralds. Cato thought there was enough money walking around the ballroom to buy Mother Hopkins the whole town of Bath, let alone one good-sized house. Just one of the necklaces or pairs of earrings, or even one of the finely worked jackets, would feed the poor children of Smithfield for a year. Truly, Mother Hopkins was never more correct when she said that life was unfair.

Suddenly Cato realized he was staring. It was a necklace he had seen before, the diamonds outshining the wearer's smile and sparkling more than any of the other jewels in the whole room.

He looked up to the wearer's face and her eyes locked with his. For a second a look of puzzlement crossed Lady Stapleton's fine pink-white face. Cato was sure she would remember the little boy in the navy-blue suit and matching turban who had vanished all those years ago. But then she smiled and turned away. Cato took a deep breath and picked up his violin.

Rowlands was nervous too. 'Did someone notice I wasn't playing?'

'This crowd would not notice a sack of gold on a dung heap,' Quarmy said as he rubbed rosin on his bow.

'It's nothing,' Cato said. He could see the Lady Elizabeth at the centre of a little group of admirers, and her diamonds shone like tiny moons.

Rowlands followed Cato's stare. 'Some necklace!' he whistled.

Quarmy was not impressed. 'My family had bronzes made by artists, which were passed down for generations. Those are merely rocks dug up from the earth and strung on thread. That woman who wears those stones is nothing, a nobody. I can read it in her every move!'

'So why then are you here playing tunes for the nobs, like the rest of us? Why are you not in the crowd dancing and laughing?' Rowlands asked.

'That is what I am asking myself at this very instant.' Quarmy tucked his violin up under his chin, and even though he pretended he was not interested in the lords and ladies, Cato could see he was by the way he scanned the crowd.

Maybe, Cato thought, he was looking for someone too. It was possible – after all, everyone had their own stories, and if Quarmy was an African prince, Cato imagined his story would be more interesting than most. Maybe it would make a good ballad: how he gained the scars across his face, how he fetched up in London. Cato was thinking there was money in the tale when he realized Quarmy was following someone with his eyes.

Cato looked out into the crowd. Quarmy was watching a beautiful young woman in a tall white fur hat, the fur so white it shone and dazzled. The young lady walked with the bearing of a princess, cutting through the crowd, and behind her followed what looked, near enough, like some Cossack soldier, also fur-hatted and with a sword that reached the floor. Behind him was a stooped black-clad elderly woman with a puff of grey hair.

'Foreigners,' Rowlands said, watching. As the young woman walked through the crowd, heads turned, and she acknowledged her admirers with a strange fierce smile.

Cato stared too.

'Magnificent!' Quarmy muttered under his breath, then looked embarrassed and turned away.

Cato smiled. 'She's the business, is she, that one?'

Quarmy cleared his throat. 'I think you'll find, if you were to converse with said lady, that she is of some family of note, of lineage.'

'Of *what* did you just say?' Rowlands asked.

'Lineage!' Quarmy sighed. 'It means breeding, family, quality.'

'Indeed, sirs.' Cato nodded and struggled to keep his face from cracking with laughter. 'I do agree she must be from a family of high renown and fame.'

And Cato told himself he wasn't lying because Mother Hopkins's family was famous throughout the City of London and beyond.

He watched as the woman in the fur hat was introduced to Sir John Stapleton, who seemed transfixed as she took off her hat and a river of bright golden curls cascaded around her shoulders. He kissed her hand and she dipped the tiniest of curtsies. There was laughter and even a ripple of applause.

Quarmy nodded approvingly. 'I would say that the lady is most definitely nobility, from the Baltic lands perhaps.'

Master Cowell was suddenly there in front of the musicians, red-faced and anxious. He tapped his baton on the nearest music stand.

'Places, gentleman, places. We have a Russian countess in our midst who has requested the Foxhall minuet! Your finest efforts, gentlemen!'

Cato picked up his bow. Bella was the centre of attention. Jack looked uneasy but stern in his Cossack uniform and Mother Hopkins had found a seat somewhere at the side of the hall.

When Cato looked through the dancers as he played, he could see Bella dancing with Sir John at the centre of the ballroom. Mother Hopkins had been right: she did make a most excellent Russian countess.

Rowlands slipped away into the night as soon as the ball was over. Cato put his fiddle into its case, turned round and he had gone.

Quarmy was dismissive. 'He will last five minutes in St Giles, that one, before he is either pressed for the navy or his master claims him. He should not have betrayed his owners. They paid good money for him.'

'And that makes the transaction fair? I think not! Have you never heard the tales of the slave ships? Of the plantations where men lose hands, feet, tongues for speaking out of turn?' Cato said.

Quarmy closed his violin case and sighed. 'If anyone is foolish enough as to let themselves be taken into capture—'

Cato was bursting with rage. 'That is not how it happens! So much money is made by those who buy and sell people, people like you and me—'

'I will speak of this no more,' said Quarmy curtly. 'You are ignorant of the fact that I know a deal more about slavery than a street musician ever could.'

Cato was shouting. 'I have been bought and sold, sir, more times than you could count. And I would not wish that experience on my worst enemy. No, sir, not even on you, who seem to have been born wearing blinkers like a carriage horse and have no idea of moving your head from left to right to even see a glimpse of the truth!'

Quarmy seemed unmoved. 'Slaves and masters. Masters and slaves. That is the order of things.'

'I assure you,' Cato said, trying to contain his anger, 'to these Englishmen, I am no different to you. They see our skin colour and put us all in the same boat, free or no, prince or slave. To the ruling classes we are nothing!'

Quarmy picked up his violin. Cato could see he was angry now, and his voice shook. *Good*, thought Cato.

'How could you think that you and I have anything in common, sir?' asked Quarmy. 'I am a prince, sir. I am a prince. My father was – no, *is*: for all I know he still lives – a king. I came here to school for a gentleman's education.'

'So why are you earning coins playing the fiddle then, Prince Quarmy? Explain that.'

Quarmy made to speak but Cato had had enough. 'No, don't tell me. I have a home to go to, a fire and a bed, and no time to listen to your inventions.'

For an instant Cato thought he saw what looked like longing pass across the haughty young man's face.

'This is an evil city for one without money,' Quarmy said, and walked away without looking back.

Cato shrugged. He had more to think about than princes. In the ballroom the white-aproned servants were back sweeping up the mess made by the nobility. Cato picked up his fiddle case and stepped out into the London night.

Up in the clear cold winter sky the stars shone like specks of diamond. The city was silver with frost and what noise there was seemed to carry pin-sharp through the brittle air: a couple of dogs barking loud enough to raise Cain in the east; somewhere in the west, metal-rimmed carriage wheels and iron-shod horses' hooves; a girl singing, her high sad voice telling of lost love. Cato thought of Rowlands, out in the cold on his first night of freedom, and of Addy cooped up in a garret in St James's.

He walked quickly, making for home across the frosted cobbles.

'You should have heard him! He was drooling all over me!' Upstairs in the parlour above The Vipers no one was asleep. Bella loosened her stays and sat down. She put on her newly minted Russian accent.

'Oh, Sir John, you are spoilink me.'

'Give it a rest, Bell,' Jack said, peeling off his knee-high boots, but Bella was still high from the dancing.

'And his missus! I've got her like that!' Bella pinched her finger and thumb together. 'She's taking me up Swallow Street tomorrow to a milliner what knows her. You'll never guess, Mother, it's only Gold and Archer's – you know, your mate Solly Gold's place! She says she simply *must* have a fur in the Russian style. She loves her threads, that Lady Stapleton!'

'Cato, you'll get over the milliner's in the morning. Let Sol know my Bella's to have a lend of whatever she likes. Tell Sol she's working and they'll be plenty in it for him, what with the Stapleton girl's custom.'

'Yes, Mother,' Cato said.

Mother Hopkins sighed. 'We needs her a house. Countess Ekaterina can't live here. Jack and Sam, you get yourselves over to Soho.'

'Don't you think Ekaterina needs something flasher than Soho, Ma?' Sam asked.

'No. She's only just arrived in town, which means she don't know London so well. Her people over in Russia—'

'In Pskoff,' Bella corrected her.

'Bless you,' Jack said.

'Leave the joking outside, Jack. Her people, they'd not know the latest news. They'd find her a ken somewhere that was fashionable ten years ago – that's the way of things. Soho it is.'

'Do mean Mr Tunnadine's house?' said Jack. 'He owes ya, remember, Ma, for that job in Epping last year when we got his horses back for him off that toad Sullivan?'

Mother Hopkins smiled. 'Joshua Tunnadine's a good old cove, and me and him have more history than you imagine. I knew him first when I was no older than you, Bella, up in London with the fair ...' Mother Hopkins looked dreamily into the fire. 'Old Joshua'll lend us his house, I reckon, if you tell him it's for me, boys.'

Tunnadine, Cato thought. He'd be the one to ask about Mother Hopkins, then.

'It's well and truly done, Ma,' Jack said, knocking back his beer.

7. A Hunt in Soho

CATO SAT tight inside the sedan chair as Jack and Sam bumped and swayed in and out of Covent Garden, through the market, with the smells of rotting vegetables and dung, past the porters' shouts and yells, westward to Soho. It was nearly noon and he'd already been to the milliner's and warned them to expect Bella, though with a new name and accent.

The sedan chair hurtled up the Tottenham Road, swerving to avoid a carriage and a party of schoolboys in long blue coats. Cato thought of Quarmy again and, looking back at the scholars, realized he'd never seen one with a black face in his whole life. Quarmy could be as much a merchant of lies and flummery as anyone else.

And Rowlands, free in name, but somewhere out in the rookeries of the parish of St Giles, where the poor slept a dozen or more to a room.

Cato knew his life with Mother Hopkins was as close to a charmed one as could be imagined for a young boy whose skin was less than porcelain white. He had thanked his stars more than once that Mother Hopkins had not discarded him as soon as they were out of Newgate, for it was more than a few years and more meals than he could count before he had begun to earn his keep. Why did she take them in, Jack and Addy and Sam? One day, he told himself, he would ask.

The chair pulled up suddenly in Soho Square. A few years ago it had been the best address in town and there were a deal of fine but, compared to St James's, slightly down-at-heel-looking houses.

'We've a job up Westminster, double pay, if we're quick,' Sam said as Cato got down from the chair.

'So we're not stopping.' Jack stamped his feet to knock the mud from his shoes. 'I tell you what, Sam,' he said. 'I'd rather we wore those high Russian boots than these damnable slippers any day of the week.'

'You chose them! Now stop working your tongue and work your feet instead,' Sam snapped. 'And, Cato, good luck with Master Tunnadine. Remind him of the horses.'

Cato decided to see if Sam knew any more about Mother Hopkins. 'I heard from some talk in The Vipers that old Josh Tunnadine was more than sweet on Mother Hopkins.'

Sam was dismissive. 'I heard half of London was sweet on her once. Come on, Jack! We're late.'

Cato watched them as they raced off, then looked around at the houses. A pair of children ran past him talking a language Cato thought must be French. He knew Soho and Spitalfields were the best places in town for French pastries when there was any spare cash to be had for them. Addy loved the ones curled like a ram's horns the best, and if she'd been at home, Cato would have bought her one.

Master Tunnadine's house was called Carfax, and was four storeys of good London brick. It must have been extremely grand not so long ago. The windows to the upper floors were shuttered and looked as if they had not been opened for years. Cato stepped up and knocked hard at the black painted door. He tried to remember Master Tunnadine but then recalled he'd never been round at The Vipers, and it was only Mother Hopkins and Sam and Jack that had had any dealings with the fellow. He did remember the Epping job and it made him shiver. The countryside was not Cato's favourite place – far too much mud.

The door squeaked open.

'Yes?'

Cato knew the voice instantly. Quarmy, tall and dark as polished ebony, had opened the door.

'Christ stripe me! The African prince! What are you doing here? You're a slave too and no mistake!' Cato had to stop himself from laughing. 'All that flim-flam about royalty!'

Quarmy held a silver tray out ready for the visitor's card, but when he saw Cato, he put it down at his side.

'I am no slave!' The fury in his answer was sharp as nails. 'And as to what I am doing here – well, not expecting you, that's true. I think you should try the servants' entrance. Whatever you want surely cannot be with Master Tunnadine.'

'I thought you was a prince!' Cato said, ignoring Quarmy and stepping inside. 'I've come to see

Master Tunnadine and you're to show me in – there's a good footman.'

Quarmy shut the front door and rolled his eyes. 'I am not a footman, and I am no slave! I am a personal valet and adviser.'

'Oh right, yes. Advise Master Tunnadine on opening doors, do you?' Cato couldn't help smiling. 'Or maybe you're teaching him music? Are you going to show me in then or not?'

'What's your business? Do you have any business?' Quarmy asked snootily.

'Naturally. I am Cato Hopkins, here on behalf of Mother Hopkins, of Covent Garden.'

For a moment Quarmy said nothing.

'*The* Mother Hopkins?'

'I do not doubt there is more than one,' Cato said – he was used to this reaction.

'You know *the* Mother Hopkins?' Quarmy lowered his voice. 'The Queen of Scoundrels? You are not lying?'

'Queen of Scoundrels? I've not heard that one before. And yes, I know her. I am her son.' Cato coughed. 'Of sorts.'

'Don't tell me!' Quarmy feigned wonder. 'There is more than one way of begetting children? Then

England is truly more wondrous than I could have imagined.'

'Adopted son.'

'Wait there. I'll tell Master Tunnadine you are here. But I need to speak with you, in private.'

Cato could not imagine what Quarmy would want with him. As he waited, he looked around. Inside, the house was smarter than outside: there were a few good paintings, although the walls were painted in darker colours than were fashionable.

Then the door to the drawing room opened and Quarmy waved Cato inside.

Master Tunnadine was folding a copy of the *London Gazette* on his lap as Cato entered. He looked older than Mother Hopkins, and was wearing a black coat with a velvet cap on his head. White tufts of hair escaped from underneath.

'Young Cato! I have not seen you since you were, ooh, six or seven years.' He put out his hand for Cato to shake.

'I was with Jack Godwin and Sam Caesar in Epping, sir. Last year,' Cato replied.

'The horses, yes, I was glad it went well! Come, sit. Close to the fire.' He gave a throaty cough.

'Tell me, what worries my Mariah so that she needs old Joshua?'

Cato sat down – *his Mariah*? He had never heard anyone refer to Mother Hopkins like that.

'I did hear the wedding lay is over now.' Mr Tunnadine put the *Gazette* down on a small table and smiled.

Cato was stunned. How did he know of that?

'And you, I can see, are grown too tall to play the pageboy.' Tunnadine leaned forward and poked at the fire in the grate. 'Mariah has mouths to feed and too many responsibilities to bank on living fast and loose with the law much longer.' He turned to Quarmy, who was standing by the door, listening hard. 'If you'd kindly leave us, Master Quarmy, I'd be more than grateful.'

Quarmy said nothing and shut the door firmly after him.

'I can see your confusions writ all across your face!' exclaimed Tunnadine. 'Mariah should have taught you to hide your feelings better than that.'

'But you seem to know all about us,' Cato protested. 'Do you know why I am here as well?'

'Mariah Hopkins and I share much history, boy. And I make it my business to know what goes on in town, as does she. So. How may I help?'

Cato explained that they needed the house as Bella's – or rather the Countess Ekaterina's – London home. Tunnadine laughed. 'That is her!' He held up the *Gazette* and Cato read: BALTIC BEAUTY CHARMS LONDON SOCIETY.

'She must have looked a picture! Little Arabella a countess! I've not seen her since she were a maid of twelve.' He sighed. 'Well, you are most welcome. But know this: Carfax, my house, is as much a sham as you or I.' Tunnadine stood up and waved Cato to follow him. 'This is not my home. For my sins I am still in Kent with my lady wife. I won Carfax off an officer in the Horse Guards regiment in a game of cards last Michaelmas. My wife would have me sell, for she is afraid of London – she says it turns my head, and to be fair she is most probably right.' He opened the door to the hall and called for Quarmy to come with a lighted candle; he descended the staircase in a flash.

'You have met, you two? You are, after all, brothers of a kind.'

'I think you'll find that I am royalty,' Quarmy said sharply. 'And Cato is not.'

'What is royalty but an accident of birth?' Master Tunnadine said, leading the way up the stairs. 'Oh, I do not doubt you are who you say you are, Master Quarmy. After all, your lineage is written across your face.'

'So he *is* a prince?' Cato asked.

'Indeed. Those scars mark out his princehood as much as any crown. But as for the rest of humanity, we are none of us entirely what we seem. For all I know young Cato may be royalty too.'

'I am not so sure about royalty, sir. Mother Hopkins always told me I was bought for pennies from a girl in Newgate Prison.'

Tunnadine turned round. 'No, no, no! That's not the tale. Your mother, for I assume it was her – indeed, she was as tawny as you – was passing Newgate, with you hidden inside a rather shabby cloak of some fustian stuff, I do recall.'

Cato was gobsmacked. 'You were there?'

'Indeed! It was my pennies that paid for you!'

'The girl, sir. Did you ask her name? Did you know her at all?'

'Of course not! I never saw the woman again. Come now, to business. This house ... You will have to tell your Mistress Hopkins that the upper floors are unusable.' Tunnadine pushed open a door and held out the candle. It was a jumble of furniture and parcels, and in the thin candlelight the dust swirled like soot.

'Mother Hopkins said that we'd need the house next week at the latest.'

'Then you'll have a deal of work getting it ready, I've no doubt. Tell her to come and see me herself and I promise I'll dragoon a team of men in here ready to do the drawing room in the finest Russian style if she thinks it will help, though Mariah will have to stump up their wages. I'd do more if I could. There's many a tale I could tell . . .' Tunnadine shook his head and smiled, remembering. 'But my Mistress Tunnadine, a most upright young woman, would have me tarred and feathered if she found any of this out.' He sighed. 'Back home in Kent I am a deacon in our country church. How's that for a pretty tale? Joshua Tunnadine, a deacon!' He shook his head. 'Times change.'

Quarmy coughed. 'Your afternoon appointment, Master Tunnadine. You will have me fetch the papers from Gray's Inn?'

'Yes, yes, I must ready myself.' The old man shuffled down the stairs, and Cato and Quarmy followed.

'So you knew Mother Hopkins well?' Cato asked.

'Better than anyone alive, I am sure,' Tunnadine replied.

'And you know about me?'

Tunnadine waved a hand. 'I have told you everything about your provenance there is to tell. Ask Mariah herself but there is no more to it than that. Now, run along and inform your mistress I wish to see her. And, Quarmy – be quick to Gray's Inn.'

Quarmy had caught up with Cato by the churchyard at St Giles. Cato wished he hadn't, for he would rather have been alone with his thoughts. The afternoon was busy even though it was cold. The sun shone on the frosted cobbles and there were plenty of beggars bundled up in rags, breathing clouds of white smoke.

Cato walked fast. He was imagining a younger Tunnadine handing over a few pennies and being passed an infant. Cato tried to imagine the face of the woman. She could have been a girl – did Tunnadine say *girl*, or *young woman*? He imagined Tunnadine trying to shush and quiet his own baby self, bawling as his mother disappeared into the stew of the city.

'Watch your step!' Cato had walked into the crossing sweeper at the top of Great White Lyon Street. He had reached the Seven Dials, and the smell of hot metal and thick ink caught in his throat. This was where the best ballads were printed. Once he'd bought one that was still hot from the press and warmed his hands as he read. And although he was in a hurry, looking in the window took no time at all.

He hadn't realized Quarmy was still beside him, looking out of breath from hurrying.

'I think you'll find Gray's Inn is better reached if you take the Oxford Road,' Cato said.

Quarmy said nothing. Instead of his usual arrogant air, he suddenly looked forlorn and morose, more like the kitten Addeline had saved from drowning last spring, just as Ezra was about to take it to meet its maker in a bucket in The Vipers' yard where the barrels were stored.

Quarmy did not move.

'Quarmy, are you quite well? Is it the cold? I expect you can't be used—'

Quarmy cut him off. 'It pains me to ask but I am in desperate need.'

'Excuse me?' said Cato, taken aback.

'I was offhand with you at our first meeting – please excuse me. You are Cato Hopkins, son of *the* Mother Hopkins?'

'I think that's clear enough, and you, as you have told me often, are a prince of Brinny, or Bonny.'

'Bonny. That's the truth. And I have been trying to find a way to Mother Hopkins these past days! I only took the post with Tunnadine because he promised me he knew her, and he has had me running errands all over town and waiting on him at his pleasure.'

Cato smiled. 'Master Tunnadine is almost as cunning as Mother Hopkins. If he had told you straight away, you would have left him to stew! And anyway, I fail to see why a prince would need any help at all. You are, as you keep telling me, a man who likes the natural order of things. Mother Hopkins is only sought by those who wish to turn the natural order on its head.'

Quarmy gulped at the air.

'One thing I do know, Quarmy, is that I cannot stand here in the street with the north wind freezing the marrow in my bones to ice.'

'Mine is a long story, sir – please do not go. Please. Listen!'

'Well, walk with me quickly. There is a good pie shop in Little White Lyon Street. If you must talk at all, let's talk there.'

Quarmy began speaking as they walked. He was a prince – he said it again. Master Tunnadine had recognized the patterns on his face that were as much a sign of royalty on the west coast of Africa, he said, as a crown and sceptre would be to Queen Anne.

'This is it.' Cato opened the door and they were engulfed by a warm fug of hot breath and tobacco smoke. A few folk turned to look a few seconds longer at the two dark-skinned boys, but that was only because they were farmers, up from the country in brown canvas smocks.

A boy around Cato's age was standing on a table at the far end of the shop singing the latest ballad, one about how he'd won the lottery but lost his love.

Quarmy had a faraway look in his eye. 'I'd be more than happy to win that lottery. It would solve all my problems at once.'

'It is a mug's game, Quarmy,' said Cato. 'The lottery serves to make the poor poorer and to part fools from their money. And you said you were a prince. You said your father had bronzes and musicians and you said you were at school! Was that all lies?'

'No. I *was* at school. I was sent down.'

'Sent down?' Cato hadn't heard the expression.

A girl much younger than Addy thumped two pies down on to the rather grubby table and held out her hand for payment.

'Farthing each!' she shouted at them over the singing.

'I have no money! Quarmy hissed. 'Why do you think I work for Tunnadine?'

The girl and Cato rolled their eyes and Cato stumped up a ha'penny. Cato picked up his pie and enjoyed the feeling of warmth seep into his cold hands.

'You said you was "sent down",' Cato said, before taking a bite.

'Expelled, thrown out,' Quarmy revealed. 'My father does not know. He has paid for five years of English education in advance and I have left after two. He would be utterly mortified. I was supposed to go on to university to study Greek and Latin. My father did not understand, and at first, neither did I. They would no sooner let an African into their precious Cambridge than make a chicken a lady-in-waiting to the Queen!'

Cato laughed and almost lost some of his pie. 'Now that I would pay to see.'

'This is serious! I was thrown out because of Ruth, thrown out and relieved of my money, my living, by her cheating father!'

Cato's face showed blankness.

'She was my schoolmaster's daughter.' Quarmy sighed. 'Prettiest girl in all of Barnet.'

Cato saw Quarmy's eyes mist over and could tell he was lost in some kind of dream. Still, he told himself, there was probably not much competition as to pretty girls in Barnet. As far as he could remember, the place was no more than a village where the ash men carted the rubbish of the city. But still, Cato could see the moonish look on the young man's face as proof of the same emotion he'd seen in young Edgar as his father dragged him away from Bella. Love. Quarmy sighed again and Cato wondered if his Ruth did love him truly – or maybe she was like Bella. Was there a way you could really tell? It could be a pile of dreams that Quarmy had staked his future on. Could a Barnet girl, one with less sophistication in her little finger than a Billingsgate fishwife, really see beyond the spiral scars and love this Quarmy – even if he was a prince?

Outside, the church clock at St Martin-in-the-Fields struck three o'clock.

'Christ swipe me! I was to be back home before now. See, Master Quarmy – or should I call you *sire*? – although you have drawn me a pretty picture of your life so far, I fail to see how I or –' Cato lowered his voice – 'Mother Hopkins could help.' Quarmy opened his mouth to go on but Cato put a hand up to stop him. 'No, please, and even if she – *we* could help, we are currently more than one hundred per cent engaged. It would be impossible.'

Cato ate up the last crumbs of his pie and stood up to leave.

'If I were in your shoes, Master Quarmy, I would work my passage on a ship back to Bonny and live the life of ease and feather beds you was born to. Oh – excepting one thing. I would take over so many guns and cannon that when the slavers came I'd pepper their ships with shot and dance as they all sank. Clear? Now, if you excuse me, I have to get on.'

Quarmy got to his feet, a half-eaten pie in hand. 'I am a prince, sir. I can no more work my passage than sweep the streets! But I have not told you the half of it! Please, sir! Wait!'

There was much work to do: errands to half of London for Mother Hopkins, more clothes for Bella to be found for an Ice Ball in Mayfair. 'Quarmy, I am sorry.' Cato smiled a half-smile and slid between the benches of the pie shop and out into the street. He heard Quarmy calling after him and felt more than a little guilty. He turned round and saw the young man standing at the door, pie in hand. He yelled at the top of his voice, pointing at Cato with his half-pie.

'Cato Hopkins! I . . . I command you!'

The imperious sound of Quarmy's voice carried down the street and Cato's guilt rose up into the cold London air like a pauper's breath and vanished. He turned and shouted back, 'Sir Prince! I think you'll find I'm not your subject!'

8. View Halloo

'SORTED, MA!' Sam said, putting his hands out to warm. There was a big pine log crackling on the fire, which scented the room and made Cato think of Christmas. 'Bella will invite the Stapletons to Carfax this next Monday. And Jack gets to put the boots on again.'

'Oh, those boots look better and better on my feet every time I wear 'em. I swear those Russkies know how to keep a body warm,' Jack said.

'Well, make sure you keep your mouth sealed shut. I don't want a word – even a sound – out of your lips that will betray you're from Islington Spa rather than St Petersburg.' Mother Hopkins looked straight at Jack.

'You can count on me, Ma. You'll not hear a squeak,' Jack said. 'And Bella's already told Elizabeth – you heard she calls her "cousin" now! – that I lost my tongue in a skirmish outside Pskoff. And she has planted the seeds of our investment opportunity.'

Mother Hopkins sucked hard on her pipe. 'Tobacco,' she said, leaning back. 'The gold that grows on trees.' She blew out a cloud of thick blue smoke.

'It's bushes, Ma, not trees,' Sam said.

'Bushes! Trees! It's God's own green leaves that turn to hard cash. And more modern than a playhouse gold mine. If you'd told me when I was your age, Cato, that we'd be playing a scheme with leaves, I'd have thought you soft-headed! Tobacco! Who'd think it?'

'And the price in the London Exchange rises almost daily,' Cato said. 'People are mad – after all, you cannot eat or wear the stuff.'

'You can't eat gold either, Cato. That's how it is, and our Bella – Ekaterina – is in London to purchase tobacco trading rights in the Baltic. She'll make the whole deal seem unmissable. I've spoken to Joshua – Master Tunnadine – and he will be our broker. He'll put a bad American wig on his bald Kentish pate and play a cove hot-foot from the colonies.' Mother Hopkins smiled. 'He's as good a man as ever lived, old Joshua Tunnadine! He'll paint up a picture so rosy the Stapletons'll be waving their goree in the air and begging he'll take it off 'em!'

For a minute, when she mentioned Tunnadine, Cato thought Mother Hopkins's eyes misted over, but it passed instantly. He wanted to ask her about Newgate, and about himself, but there were too many people around, and Jack and Sam would only rib him about it. He sighed and inched closer to the warmth of the fire.

'What're you sighing for, Cato?' Jack asked. 'Lost love? Laziness, more like. I know you – you're needing a bit more of the action. Or maybe you're troubling yourself about tomorrow night?'

Cato sat up straight. 'No, never! It'll make a change from nights sat in while you lot gad about playing Russians.'

'He wants a go of your boots, Jack,' Sam said, laughing.

'Wearing a pair of fancy boots is a deal easier than breaking into a body's business. In the dark!' Cato was indignant.

Mother Hopkins leaned down to where he was sitting by the fire and ruffled his hair. Cato pulled away and then, for a quick second, wished he hadn't.

'You're a good lad,' she said. 'There's not a boy in town could get in among Sir John's accounts as fine or as fast as you. Addy'll let you in by the area door and you're to be in and out quicker than a dog down a rat hole. We know they'll be at the ball with Bella till past midnight.' Mother Hopkins looked hard at Cato.

'Are you sure it's not too much of a risk for nothing, Ma? I mean, we know they're loaded,' Sam said.

Mother Hopkins tapped the side of her nose. 'There's rich folk and rich folk, and there's some that do a mighty good job of *looking* like rich folk. No point in us wasting our precious time taking down a pair of coves who are all front with nothing in the bank. What if all the cash went on that fancy house?'

Sam and Jack nodded.

'And, Cato, mind you tell our Addeline our thoughts are with her. Now, you should get along to your bed and dream of barrel locks and Dutch teeth, or whatever it is those infernal things are called. And, Jack and Sam, have a mind to look for Bella. She should be at home now, not out gallivanting in borrowed clothes. You go and fetch her home please. Go! I need my thinking time.'

Cato got up in a hurry. Mother Hopkins liked her thinking time uninterrupted. He was climbing the stairs on his way to bed when he heard Jack and stopped still.

'One thing, Ma, before we go. Old Ezra said as how he'd seen one leery-looking cove hanging about The Vipers like a bad smell the last day or so, and he was there again this afternoon when we came in from town.'

Cato stood stock-still on the stairs and listened as hard as he could.

'Ezra said he was pacing about on the street outside like he wanted something badly but didn't know how to ask, or, worse, like he was being paid to watch us. Although, if someone is paying him, it can't be much on account of how he sticks out like a man looking for a wife down Haymarket. Blacker than Sam, he was, but with these patterns all over his face like he was, I dunno, like he was embroidered . . .'

Cato slipped into the area of the Stapletons' house. His feet were chilled in his soft-soled slippers; under his coat his lock picks and tools were rolled up in a case of yellow leather. He knew the parish watchman was still on the far side of the square, where Sam Caesar had engaged him in conversation about the excessive number of foreigners working on the building sites that seemed to have sprung up in every corner of the city. He hadn't bumped into Quarmy – and from Jack's description Cato was sure it had been *him* hanging around outside The Vipers – even though he had spent most of the day watching out for him.

Cato knocked twice on the area door, firmly but softly. Addy must have been waiting there because the door was opened in a second. Cato tried not to gasp, because even in the pale moonlight that filtered down into the basement he could see she looked tired. Her shoulders drooped and the fierce set of her chin was somehow less fearsome. Even her hair was smoothed back into submission.

She put a hand to his mouth. 'Don't say anything. I know I'm a state.'

'I never—'

'Cato Hopkins, I can read your face quicker than you read a ballad sheet,' Addy hissed. 'I can't wait till this damnable lay is done with. Whatever you do, Cato, never, ever go into service, not for all the gold in Threadneedle Street. Come on upstairs, and don't tread on the fourth step up. It creaks like Mother's bones on a rainy day!'

Cato followed Addeline silently up to the first floor, keeping his eyes on the familiar curve of her back. When they reached the landing, she opened a door for him and stood aside.

'I'll wait out here. If you hear any sound, you know the game's up. And for God's sake be quick.' She leaned over and passed him a candle stub on a saucer, then kissed him. For a second Cato thought her face softened; he felt himself flush hot and was glad there was no light from the curtained and shuttered windows.

He heard the door close behind him and suddenly it was dark. He lit the candle and the room flickered into life.

Cato knew where to go: the small blond-wood bureau with an inlaid pattern of a rose in darker wood. The outer door opened easily and he flipped the writing desk top down to reveal several small drawers and cubby holes. None of them moved and, to cap it all, there were no keyholes. Cato cursed under his breath.

He had heard much of these modern cabinets: no visible locks, but secret sprung mechanisms that opened to a touch, if you knew where to touch, that is. But he'd only ever seen one, only ever practised on one.

Cato took a deep breath and ran his hands under the drawers at the back of the desk. Nothing moved.

He leaned over and felt all around the back of the bureau, moving his fingers very slowly but with an even pressure. Suddenly he was aware of a depression in the wood, a place where he could press harder, and then there was the softest of cracking sounds before a deep, heavy drawer slid open under his eyes as if by magic.

Cato smiled. Sometimes there was no better feeling in the world than beating a lock.

Inside, a roll of papers, some envelopes sealed with carbuncles of red wax, navy leather-bound inventories of the house in London and the house in Hampshire, of the farms and estates in England and in the Caribbean; lists of acreage and cattle; lists of furniture, of paintings, silver and jewellery; and after all that lists of people, of Negroes, of men, women and children. These were only things to the Stapletons, just like the fine wooden bureau Cato sat at in the dark.

The names were numerous: Jupiter, Tom Turkey, Femmy, Oxford, Glasgow. Just reading them, Cato was aware of a knot growing in his stomach and he thanked God and Mother Hopkins that his life was not theirs.

He closed the inventory book. He had business. Quickly he flicked through as much as he could, looking for signs of bad debts, but there were none. The Stapletons' wealth was as solid as the dome on the new cathedral. Mother Hopkins would be pleased.

The door opened and Cato felt his heart jump up into his throat.

'Are you done?'

It was only Addy, whispering.

'You could have stopped my heart!' he hissed back at her.

Addeline came inside and shut the door behind her. 'Have you finished? Only I been counting – I got up to five hundred. You should be done by now.' She sat down on a chair. 'I am so tired.'

'Nearly done.' Cato shut the drawer and pushed the bureau back against the wall slowly and silently. 'There. No one'll know I've been,' he said.

Addy yawned. 'It's not just the work, Cato! I miss The Vipers so much it's like I feel sick to my stomach all the time.'

Cato thought she looked thin. 'You must eat, Addeline. You need your strength. You'll be home soon, you know that.' He checked the desk was exactly as it had been. 'And you can get straight to your bed now.'

'You know, that's the only comfort there is in this place. I tell you clear, I ain't never working for no one in service ever, ever again.' Addy pushed herself up off the chair and opened the door to the landing. Suddenly, from the street, there was a clattering of hooves and iron wheels. Addy ran back and looked between the curtains and out through the crack in the shutters.

'Don't worry, Cato, it won't be for the Stapletons. That's not their horses, nor their carriage neither.'

Cato nodded.

'Hang on! The cove's only getting down and coming here!' She blew out the candle and the room was in darkness again. There were shouts from below and someone thumping on the front door as if their life depended on it. Cato and Addy froze.

More knocking and shouting. They could hear it from the first floor.

'A message for the Stapleton household! Open up with all speed, I beg you! Good people, terrible news! News from the country!'

Cato looked at Addy, but there was so little light in the room he could only imagine her face mirrored the shock in his own. He took a deep breath. 'He's not going to come up here, Addy.'

But Addy just said, 'Hide!' and she was gone from his side. Cato felt his way around the room. There was a couch against the wall and he threw himself under it. He heard Addy slip through the door on to the landing and then a great deal of thumping and running up and down stairs. Whatever was happening, the whole house seemed to be awake now – ribbons of yellow light showed under the door, more footsteps thumped. He tried to turn and banged his elbow into the wall. Then it seemed like hours before he heard the handle turning; he held his breath until he was sure it was Addy.

She hustled him down the stairs and into the front area. Whenever he opened his mouth to ask her what was going on, she shushed him.

'You have to go! The Stapletons are called home from the dance.'

'But the coach. It's in the square. Someone will see.'

'I'll go up first and talk to the driver – you run the other way,' she said hurriedly.

'What's happening?'

'Old man Stapleton is dead. Our Sir John's a bleedin' marquess now. They'll be insufferable,' she complained. 'Come on.'

Outside it had started snowing. Addy let Cato out of the house into the silent square. The carriage was being led away into the mews and the falling snow made a useful curtain. It would be hard to see a boy slip through the area gate, and any footsteps he left on the new yellow stone pavement would be covered almost instantly. Cato found Sam Caesar waiting at the corner of the square and they both started walking briskly back to The Vipers. As they turned into Piccadilly, the Stapletons' flash brougham pulled by matching greys passed, going the other way at double speed, one horse almost slipping on the frozen road.

'They're back in a hurry. What happened?' Sam asked. 'I saw the coach and pair arrive earlier – he was driving like he had a ghost on his tail.'

'I s'pose he did, in a manner of speaking,' said Cato. 'Old man Stapleton, our Stapleton's father the marquess, died this afternoon up in the country.'

'Mother Hopkins won't like it. She likes a lay to go nice and smooth.'

Cato pulled his coat close and hurried to keep up with Sam. 'She can't stop the dead from dying though. And look on the bright side – they might be swimming up to their necks in even more cash!'

Sam was quiet for a while before he spoke. 'So much cash that a couple of fields of tobacco won't mean so much as a fig. And they'll be so busy with the mourning and that, they won't want Bella spouting cod Russian in their ears.' He sighed.

Cato thought Sam might be right, but he didn't answer. There was a knot in his middle just below his ribs and above his stomach. This lay was on the wrong road for success, he was sure of it. He wanted it all to be over and done with and Addy to come home. He shivered, and it wasn't just the thickly falling snow.

The streets were still busy enough that no one paid them any attention, and the snow meant no one stopped to wonder what two young black men were doing out at this ungodly hour.

Cato was more pleased than usual when they turned the corner into Great Queen Street and saw the lights burning in the windows of the Nest of Vipers. The snow had begun to settle and The Vipers' sign creaked under the extra weight.

It was a relief to be home. Cato stamped the snow off his feet and took himself upstairs. Mother would be waiting and he'd have to break the bad news, but at least there'd be a warm drink and a hot fire.

Upstairs, Mother Hopkins was sitting in her chair by the fire. The smell of tobacco filled the room, but through the smoke Cato could see that the look on her face was dark as thunder. Maybe she'd heard about the death – or perhaps it was worse: Bella had been unmasked; the magistrates had put her in the Westminster lock-up and were on their way.

He looked at Sam, neither of them wanting to speak first.

'There's news, Mother,' Cato said as he took off his jacket. 'Old man Stapleton is dead—' He stopped.

'We've company,' Mother Hopkins said, and suddenly Cato realized he was looking at Quarmy, sitting by the fire in the upstairs room of The Vipers, firelight shining on his skin as if he'd sat there all his life.

'And more than that,' she said. 'Master Tunnadine is called back to Kent.'

No wonder she looked grim, Cato thought.

Mother Hopkins refilled her pipe. 'And if the old marquess is dead, in one night our world is changed, turned upside down. All plans must be remade. We'll need more than the promise of another fortune to reel these fishes in.'

It was hours later when Cato led Quarmy down the stairs and out of The Vipers. Although it was not yet dawn, the city was beginning to wake up, the first rattles of market traders pushing barrows west to Covent Garden. The snow that had fallen all night made everything seem clean and sparkling, as if London was a place where only good deeds and kind thoughts flourished. All the dirt and sin scoured clean away – or rather covered in a blanket of shining white. The reflecting snow gave the still dark early morning a strange lightness, an unearthly, unreal glow, and the harsh cold sent those poor souls who slept in doorways straight to heaven or hell.

Quarmy was tired but walked out into the street, head held high as if reviewing his courtiers rather than making for Soho Square. He turned and waved.

'I knew Mother Hopkins would help,' he said.

Cato wanted to answer that all was not over yet, and counting chickens before they were hatched was always a bad idea. He bolted the front door behind Quarmy and made his way back up the stairs. Addeline would be getting up, lighting the fires, as he made for his bed. Too much had happened in one night. Not only was there a death in the Stapleton family, but Master Tunnadine would no longer play the inside man for them, the tobacco baron home from Virginia with investment opportunities a-plenty. His wife had heard he might be falling in with his old, and not entirely straightforward, lifestyle.

Quarmy had brought the bad news that Tunnadine had gone and then petitioned Mother Hopkins. He wanted help with his schoolmaster, who was refusing his daughter's hand in marriage while holding on to his funds so Quarmy could neither return to Africa nor set himself up in London as he wished.

Mother Hopkins had said nothing, just scowled and sucked on her pipe. Cato had seen it all before. This was her way: she would think good and hard. Cato sighed as his head hit the pillow. They had spent so much cash and time on this lay. If they cut and ran now, there would be even more money to be found before Mother Hopkins could think about Bath.

He was drifting into sleep, imagining meeting Addy coming home from the Stapletons' – surely she would be allowed home now – when the door creaked open and Mother Hopkins came in. Cato sat up suddenly.

'I need a word,' she said, and opened the curtain so that the first daylight came in.

'With me, Ma? I know I met that Quarmy, but I thought he wasn't quite watertight, so I said we couldn't help, that we was too busy—'

'Hush up, Cato. That young man's problems aren't what's troubling me.'

Mother Hopkins looked out of the window at the city. She sighed. 'I'll miss this town and all that's in it, and that's the truth.'

'But the Stapletons . . . they'll be in mourning.'

'Death is never an excuse to stop living, Cato.' Mother Hopkins sat on the end of the bed. 'And there is always better work to do than sleeping.'

'I don't understand, Mother. Tunnadine's out of it.' As Cato spoke the name, it seemed as if a shadow moved across Mother Hopkins's face. He went on, 'What I mean is, we've no inside man. Jack can't do it – they think he's a mute Russian –

Sam can't do it in case the Lady Elizabeth recognizes him . . .'

Mother tutted. 'There's always more than one way to skin a cat, or part a greedy man from his gold. Always see the opportunity, Cato, not the impediment. No doubt our Stapletons will come into a deal more cash. I know the old man had more holdings in West India than the Governor of the Bank of England himself . . .'

Cato made to speak but Mother put up her hand. 'Rich people, greedy people, they never have enough goree. Even if they can furnish their houses with beaten gold, they'll always want something more, especially if it seems like they're cutting corners, getting something no one else has. That's what we have to be giving them! And the way I see it, with young Sir John – or should I say, the new Marquess of Byfield – busy with sorting his father's estate, we can cut straight to the chase, straight to the softest cheese in the dairy, in a manner of speaking.'

'You mean the Lady Elizabeth?' Cato asked.

Mother Hopkins nodded. 'She's the way in, and with her husband out of the picture Bella can wrap her round her little Russian finger. I thought about this . . . Bella's so close to that

Elizabeth, you couldn't slide one of Addeline's playing cards in between 'em. It's too good an opportunity – we're too close to the cash.'

'But Lady Elizabeth won't be interested in investments surely? From what Bella says she cares only for herself – how her hair is dressed, what to wear for which dance.'

'Too right, Cato, too right.' Mother Hopkins nodded. 'She follows fashion closer than the starved crow follows the plough. And that's how we'll bait our hook.'

Cato was confused. He got up and put on his jacket for warmth.

'*Fashion*,' Mother Hopkins said. 'The finest silks and satins, fresh from the east. So beautiful, so rare, so far ahead of the weavers of London or Paris with their patterns and their subtleties! I can see 'em now in my mind's eye. Complete originals and all at knock-down prices!'

Cato smiled, bowed low and pretended to lay out a bolt of cloth. 'Yes, madam – unrivalled quality, unparalleled beauty.'

Mother Hopkins nodded. 'Thank you kindly, sir. I'll have the lot!'

'But are you sure that'll make enough of a return, Ma: some cloth for dresses?'

'We'll make it enough. Oh, it won't be no ordinary cloth – you wait and see. We'll throw some jewels and gold in with the silks. And we'll make the whole package too good to be true!' she said. 'And you know what else, Cato? I can see a way your friend can be a real help to us with this.'

'He ain't my friend. He believes in the natural order of things, I reckon, as his father makes more cash selling people than anything else.'

'You don't know that for certain, Cato. We can do each other a deal of good. He is a prince. The genuine article, not some faker. He can be our inside man.'

'Mother, no! He can't tell a lie to save his life, and he has such arrogance he'd never work for us!' Cato protested. The thought of Quarmy helping them was too much to bear.

'That's what you'll teach him,' Mother said. 'You'll show him what he's to do, tell him when to open his mouth and when to keep it shut. You'll be his valet, you'll be his brains. It's ideal!'

'But, Mother, you don't know him. He'll never listen to me – I am a mere peasant as far as he's concerned. And I don't know, Ma, but there's something . . . something not right. Are you sure that Quarmy's what he says he is? I mean, I know he talks flash . . .'

Mother Hopkins smiled. 'Joshua knew what he was doing. Here.' She took out a letter rolled up tight in her pocket. 'Tunnadine wanted a manservant and Quarmy did the job. He lived with the boy – what you see is what you get.' She put the letter back in her pocket.

'I can see your worry, but don't fret so, Cato. Quarmy needs hard cash, and he can earn it and do us a favour at the same time. I have no intention of running a scam against his old teacher or embroiling ourselves in more trouble than is necessary.' Mother Hopkins stood up. 'He is a prince! His father is a king! A king who trades with the east. Bella said the Lady Elizabeth is one for the fashion, for clothes and fripperies, and that's the way to her pocket, I fancy.' Her eyes came alive at the thought. 'Oh, he'll spin us tales and we can use that in so many ways. He'll worm his way into Lady Elizabeth's finances and we'll have the Stapletons and the house in the west before the year is done! We have to make this lay the best we've ever set. We'll be playing for our lives now, Cato. Just you remember that!'

9. A Sudden Change of Horses

CATO WALKED with Quarmy across Covent Garden Market and down towards the river. They were both wearing their best clothes. Quarmy was got up in a suit that reeked of wealth. It was, he said, the last one his father had had made for him and the only thing of value he'd taken from his trunk at school. Cato wore his Sunday best, which paled into insignificance next to Quarmy's. His suit was now a little small around the armpits, and he thought that if he raised his arms, the seams would split. He patted his jacket pocket to make sure the cards Mother Hopkins had had newly printed were ready and waiting.

Mother Hopkins had told him to 'open Quarmy's eyes and give him as thorough an education in the trade of deceit as was possible'. The snow had now turned to slush and filth, yellow with horse pee in places and grey with dirt everywhere else. The traders – and there were fewer than usual on account of the weather – were packing up their empty baskets and loading truculent ponies, hooves bagged with sacking so as not to slip.

The boys crossed the Strand and followed an alley down to a set of stairs that led to the river, where the fair was still in full swing. Cato stopped.

'I want one thing clear as crystal,' he said. 'There's to be no commands. No *do this*, *do that*. Me an' you are equals now.'

Quarmy rolled his eyes.

Cato went on, 'I am not your subject, I am your teacher. Although how Mother Hopkins expects me to set you on the same road as all of us in just one day only the Lord himself knows, and that's the truth.'

'I can assure you it will come naturally to me,' said Quarmy. 'I was at the top of my class at school, and anyway, I do not need to know how to act like a prince, I am one already!'

'You do not understand at all, Quarmy. What we do is not the real world. The real world is out there in the filthy streets. We are more than real, better than real. You need to be not just a prince, but more like what somebody *thinks* a prince should be like.'

Quarmy looked confused. 'You talk complete rot!'

Cato put his hand to his forehead. 'Right, I'm talking rot, am I? How do you think we make our living? By doing good turns?'

'Of course not!' Quarmy said. 'I know what the lot of you are – coney catchers, in the common canting tongue, though of course it pains me to use it.'

'Shout it to the world, why don't you? Look, Quarmy,' Cato said. 'Remember Bella at that dance? The Russian countess? Even you thought she was a proper nob, not some girl from Covent Garden dressed up to the nines.'

Quarmy said nothing.

'You were fooled and no mistake!'

Quarmy looked slightly sheepish.

'Anyway, there's one more thing I want to ask you,' Cato continued. 'Your old man . . .'

'Old man?'

'Father . . . the king, or whatever it is you call him. He sells people, don't he?'

'I am not talking about this now: we will only argue. You don't understand what it is like in Africa.' Quarmy turned away.

'I know one thing,' Cato said. 'I know people are all the same – black, white, old, young. We're all greedy and we all don't care about other people as much as we should. Just answer me. Your pa, he sells slaves?'

Quarmy squirmed. 'My father, yes. But it is not that simple.'

'If I lived in your country, I would overthrow your father and build a bloody great cannon to fire at the slavers,' said Cato in disgust.

Quarmy laughed. He laughed all the way down to the river while Cato got more and more angry.

'You are so young, Cato. Nothing can be solved that simply. As you say, people are greedy, and guns, on the whole, seem to make things worse because no matter how many guns we Africans have, the white men always have more.'

They had reached the ice. Cato looked around. He would have to calm down. Anger was useless when he was working – it got in the way of playing and schemes.

He took a deep breath. There was work to do.

'This place is prime. Fairs always are – full of fancy and robbers and rogues and those with money burning holes in their pockets.'

'So what do you propose?' Quarmy asked.

'First off we need to find ourselves a punter, a mark; someone whose face shows the greed inside, because – and this is our number-one rule – you cannot cozen an honest man ... or woman for that matter. They'll do half the work for you if they think you're giving them something for nothing. You tell them how clever they are; how beautiful or gracious—'

'Even if they are not?'

'Yes, even if they are not. You have to be whatever they want you to be.'

'But I am a prince!'

'You worked for Master Tunnadine, didn't you? You opened the door for him and played valet? Prince or slave, it's no odds. Just button your lip and watch me.' Cato turned away and started through the crowd. He muttered under his breath, 'God strike me down if I can teach this one anything.'

'But, Cato, don't you find your conscience in any way troubled?'

Cato turned and faced Quarmy. 'I am not the one whose livelihood is earned on the broken backs of slaves!'

'You repeat yourself like a mewling child who has learned a new idea,' Quarmy said arrogantly. 'That bores me.'

Cato glared at him. '*My* conscience is clear. Like I said, we never take an honest man.' He stopped suddenly. He thought of Edgar, the poor bridegroom, for a second. He would be over Bella by now, wouldn't he? Sighing loudly, he led Quarmy through the crowd.

They'd just walked past the dancing bear and the hog roast when Cato spotted a young man wearing a particularly fine worsted jacket cut in the modern fashion. It was covered with silver embroidery and enough Dutch lace spilling out from the cuffs to make nightgowns for an entire Chelsea boarding school. Cato saw him watching an old lady wrapped up in woollens to keep out the cold; then he saw him help the woman over a slide in the ice as he cut and concealed the woman's purse, smiling at her all the time.

'See him?' Cato nudged Quarmy in the ribs. 'There, by the Spanish tumblers. For Christ's own sake don't stare! See how he moves? He is like us, watching for somebody.' He turned away. 'I have not seen that cutpurse in town before, and by the looks of him he is one that values both his appearance and his tailor.'

'You will steal from the thief?' Quarmy asked.

'Not steal, sir, never steal. The trick is to get your quarry to hand over the goods willingly; to give you the goods or the cash with a grateful heart.'

Cato turned back to the cutpurse and watched as the young man's eyes darted through the crowd before settling on a pair of shop girls carrying baskets of ribbons and fixings.

'Engage those girls in conversation, quickly! And make it plausible,' Cato said.

'What? What should I say?'

'Think on your feet, man! Put a smile on your face and be charming. Be more than charming, be regal. Tell them they shall be queens of the coast of Bonny! Make sure they know who you are.'

'But—'

'But nothing! And keep talking until I give you the say-so. Right, I will return with the cutpurse and when I do, remember this: just repeat the end of my sentence. So if I say "yes", agree most uncommonly.'

'And if you say no?'

'Then you say no! Now, watch and learn, Quarmy, watch and learn.'

Cato sent Quarmy towards the girls and took out of his pocket the pick he carried with him just in case. Then he walked towards the young man, speeding up as he neared him until he ran into the cutpurse so hard he knocked him over. Cato made sure he fell too, and for a second while he rolled into him he hooked into the silver embroidery on the young man's coat. Then he stood up, shouting curses into the crowd at the imaginary child who'd been so uncouth as to knock the pair of them down.

'Blessed city urchins!' Cato turned to the young man and helped him up, brushing him down and tugging at the embroidery a little more.

'Are you unharmed? Please pardon me, I am not from these parts. I am a humble visitor, with my master, the Prince of Bonny,' Cato said, indicating Quarmy.

'I am unhurt. I think,' the cutpurse said.

'Oh, but your jacket! See the silver threads! They are undone here.' Cato pointed at the back of the jacket, where he'd managed to pull a few threads loose in the tumble.

'God's teeth! No! This was but newly made!' cried the man.

'My master – my master could engage a tailor and put it right, no doubt. I do feel I am to blame.' Cato bowed as humbly and as low as possible. 'Let me enquire of the prince – he is a most gracious and generous master.'

Cato bowed again and led the way to where Quarmy was still making small talk with the shop girls.

'Your Highness!' Another bow. Quarmy smiled and nodded.

The shop girls giggled.

'Ooh la! You are a prince, ain't yer?' said one.

'He is an' all,' added the other.

Cato coughed. 'Excuse me, sire. Unfortunately I have damaged this gentleman's fine coat. See, the threads are loose.' He plucked at them and they unravelled more, and the young man winced as they undid.

'A very fine coat,' Cato enthused. 'Much like the one your father has purchased for you, wouldn't you say?'

'Indeed, quite so,' Quarmy said with genuine disdain. Obviously the thought that a cutpurse could wear a similar jacket to a prince was irksome, thought Cato.

The young man looked at Quarmy and took him in. 'You are, in truth, a prince?'

'Of the most ancient and venerable Kingdom of Bonny,' Cato said on Quarmy's behalf, bowing exaggeratedly.

'Is that some African isle?' asked the young man.

Quarmy was haughtily dismissive. 'Not an isle, sir, not an isle. An isle is surrounded by sea and thus, by definition, small. Our land extends into the heart of the great continent of Africa itself.'

Cato smiled.

'So you have coins enough to fix up my coat?' the cutpurse asked.

'It is but a trifle to the prince, sir,' Cato said.

'Of course. I mean my retainers to do no harm to the inhabitants of this … this small island,' Quarmy said, and Cato had to struggle to keep his face from breaking into too wide a smile.

'His Highness is staying in town … in St James's Square.' Cato pulled a card from inside his jacket. 'His Highness's card.'

The cutpurse took it and nodded. 'A good address. I myself am newly come up to town from Bath.'

'Bath?' Quarmy said without being prompted. 'I have long thought about a visit to take the waters.'

'It would be a pleasure to instruct you on my home's delights.' The cutpurse bowed low. I bet it would, Cato thought. He could see the thief was imagining that this could be the beginning of a profitable friendship. The cutpurse took off his jacket and handed it to Cato.

'Leave it with us,' Cato said. 'You may send your man round for it in the morning. Or indeed call yourself if you would wish and take some coffee.'

'It would be my pleasure,' Quarmy agreed.

'You are too kind, too kind,' said the man eagerly.

Cato bowed again and, keeping a tight hold on the coat, walked ahead of Quarmy through the crowd. After they had gone a little way he looked again and, when he was sure the man wasn't watching, urged Quarmy into a run. The coat was heavy, and the embroidery exquisite. It was only unpicked a little and Bella could make it good in no time. Cato wished he could keep it rather than hand it over to Mendes, although he was bound to give them a most excellent price.

They reached The Vipers out of breath from running.

'That was the most diverting morning I have spent for many weeks!' Quarmy said.

'That, Quarmy, is our life.' Cato checked the street behind them. 'And he has not followed us. Good.'

'Good indeed! I think I may have enjoyed myself a little too much!'

'The words flowed freely from you, that's the truth,' Cato said as they went upstairs.

Quarmy laughed. 'I think that I shall prefer playing a prince to actually being one!'

10. A New Play

CATO WOKE with a start. He'd been dreaming about a dark place, a place where he couldn't see his hand in front of his face or smell anything other than illness and death. He rubbed the sleep from his eyes and shook the thoughts away. Too many of Mother Hopkins's tales of Newgate Prison, he told himself. He stretched, and on the floor between his bed and Sam's empty one a shape moved. Cato reminded himself it was Quarmy, who would wake as soon as the bell of St Andrew's started chiming and complain that he'd had the worst night of his life, worse even than the nights he'd spent in a barn outside Friern Barnet after he'd been sent down from school.

'So this is the day!' Quarmy said and yawned. 'I'll not let you down. I'll be the best prince yet, and our ship—'

'The *Favourite*,' Cato reminded him.

'Yes indeed, that famous vessel loaded down with silks and satins from China and—'

'India!' Cato said. 'And woven a thousand times more skilfully than the nimblest Spitalfields weavers.'

'Yes, yes, from the coast of Coro ... Coro ... ?'

'Coromandel!' Cato sighed. 'You are supposed to be a scholar – can you not remember any of it?'

Last night they had stayed up long after the inn had closed, going over and over the plans for today. Cato shivered. He had worked up a sweat in the night and now the cold settled on him.

'It will come to me, I have no doubt,' Quarmy reassured him. 'Just as a violin melody works its way into my fingers before I have to play.'

'I hope so, Quarmy, for both our sakes. Not to mention the wrath of Mother if it doesn't!'

Tunnadine had left the keys for Carfax, and Bella and Mother Hopkins had spent the greater part of the previous day arranging a drawing room and dressing it for Elizabeth Stapleton's visit.

Instead of an impromptu meeting with a tobacco grower, there would now be a most entertaining and enlightening morning cup of chocolate with a real African prince in attendance.

Cato brushed down Quarmy's jacket and then his own. He would be the prince's retainer, required to say little, but carrying the important documentation regarding a ship. A special ship, the *Favourite*, run aground off the prince's kingdom and being refitted at this very moment.

The prince would beg Ekaterina, Countess of Pskoff, and Lady Stapleton to help him dispose of her cargo – one of best Indian chintz and the latest Chinese silks, so beautifully woven and dyed that London had yet to see such fabric. And all, of course, at extremely favourable rates.

Cato took a deep breath. He wished Addy was here – she would tell him not to worry. But he reminded himself he'd rather be a princely retainer than a housemaid. This plan would work.

The inn was quiet when he left with Quarmy. Sam was out, and Jack, Bella and Ma were gone to Carfax House. The rush in the bar had died down before lunch time and The Vipers seemed unnaturally sad and sullen – like Addy in a sulk, Cato thought.

Cato had wanted to wear the cutpurse's jacket. It fitted him so well, but he would have outshone Quarmy. More importantly, they'd needed the money it had made at the second-hand clothes merchant.

They had reached the Charing Cross Road when suddenly Cato was aware that Quarmy was shaking. He seemed to have frozen in the middle of the road, slack-jawed and wide-eyed.

Cato caught his sleeve. 'Quarmy, come on,' he said.

Quarmy didn't move.

'We are in the middle of the highway. Christ's blood, man, move!'

Cato took his shoulders and had to push him out of the way of the Highgate coach. 'Quarmy!'

'Ruth,' Quarmy said, softly the first time; then he shouted, 'Ruth!'

Cato followed Quarmy's eyes and saw a girl in a woollen shawl and a dark red skirt disappear down the alley to St Giles. Suddenly, like a hare zigzagging across a field, Quarmy was off after her. Cato had only seen her face for a second, and he had to admit that against the background of her rather showy red silk dress her face was round and pale. Unremarkable, he thought, and not a face to inspire the passion that seemed to have Quarmy in its grip. Cato took a deep breath and followed fast.

St Giles's struck eleven as Cato ran into the alley after Quarmy. They were supposed to be at the house; they were supposed to be there crossing the square right now, ready to knock at the door so that Jack could show them in wearing his Cossack boots.

'Quarmy!' Cato yelled. The alley was empty. Apart from some builders shivering on a wooden scaffold there was no one. As Cato ran on, the alley opened into the churchyard and he spotted the girl in the shawl hurrying out the other side and into another street.

Quarmy was catching her up, calling her name, all princely manners forgotten. At one point he slipped on a paving stone and Cato winced, imagining the slush and the dirt splashed down Quarmy's best coat.

Cato ran too. He crossed Seven Dials – for a prince, Quarmy had a fair turn of speed – and saw Quarmy's back disappear into a court off Castle Street. Cato turned the corner and ran slap into the prince, who was standing stock-still in front of a tall, thin, mean-looking house that stuck out like a broken tooth in an otherwise healthy mouth.

'Ruth!' Quarmy wailed up at the house.

Cato could see that many of the windows were lacking glass.

'Quarmy.' He took the prince's arm. 'We must get back. We are late!'

Quarmy pulled away. 'I must go to her. Ruth!' He thumped on the door and it fell open. He looked at Cato. 'I have to go. I have to see her. A few moments. Grant me that, then I will play the prince with all my heart,' he promised.

Cato stood aside. There was no point forcing him in this state. Quarmy went into the dark of the hall and vanished inside the house.

Cato waited. In the house opposite an old woman sat at the window, watching, and he smiled at her. A few moments later there was still nothing. No sound, no word; it was as if the house had eaten up and swallowed both Ruth and Quarmy. Cato stamped his feet with impatience. He should never have let Quarmy out of his sight. With so little time to spare and the prince nowhere to be seen, he approached the house and stepped inside.

The floor was rotten in places and Cato moved slowly. From the back room he could hear a low whimpering but through the crack in the door he could see nothing. He hesitated before he heard a louder noise, one that sounded like Quarmy. A soft, low 'No' came from above.

Cato would have run upstairs but he could see places where the banister had fallen away so he hugged the wall and took his time. On the first floor a door was hanging open and there was Ruth, silhouetted against a curtainless window, her round-moon face defiant and happy, in the embrace of a young man. It took Cato a second look to realize it was not Quarmy.

Ruth spoke and her voice was hard. 'If you are some acquaintance of Quarmy, could you take him away and get it into his fat black head that I want no more to do with him?'

Quarmy was leaning against the wall by the door, out of breath yet strangely still, as if the stuffing had been knocked out of him. As if he might cry. All his usual arrogance was gone.

'Quarmy . . .' Cato tried to lead him away.

Ruth and the young man were both smiling and Cato could not help but feel deeply for Quarmy. It was like the Fleet wedding all over again, as he had feared. He took Quarmy by the elbow and the prince hardly reacted, only speaking her name once more as a sad whisper: 'Ruth.'

'She is not worth a half of you. Prince or no, no man deserves that,' Cato said to him as they reached the bottom of the stairs.

'I thought she loved me!' Quarmy sobbed.

Cato imagined she had loved his money – which must have paid for the dress – rather than anything else. Back out in the street, Quarmy seemed utterly deflated.

Cato tried to steer him into an inn, thinking that maybe a sip of brandy down his throat – better still a half-bottle – would change his spirits.

'I am ruined,' Quarmy said, and Cato could see the tears welling in his eyes.

'You are a prince!' Cato tried to buoy him up. 'You are above such petty vagaries of the heart as love! Think on that!'

'Alas, I can only think of Ruth! I am no use to you now, Cato, no use at all.' He slumped against a wall and buried his face in his hands.

'Surely not!' Cato said in as jovial a tone as he could summon up, but inside he was thinking it would take the output of an entire distillery to change Quarmy's mind.

The snow started to fall again. Quarmy was right: he was utterly useless in this state. But what could Cato do now? Send Quarmy home and take a message to Mother Hopkins saying the game was up? No.

'Quarmy, Quarmy, man – perhaps you could hold a straight face and say nothing at all?'

Quarmy sighed deeply. 'I cannot tell.' A few tears rolled silently down his face.

They walked a few steps. The snow was falling harder and the buildings and the city itself was starting to be obscured by a curtain of snowflakes.

'Tell you what then, Quarmy, give me your coat. Your wig and hat too!'

'Pardon?' said the prince, looking at Cato in confusion.

'Maybe this prince's servant is now lost, or forgotten – or I will think of it on the way. Just give me your coat and hat and get back to The Vipers.' Cato took a deep breath. '*I* will be the prince now.'

11. Royalty

CATO STOOD up as straight as he could. The jacket was a little large across the shoulders and he was afraid it might make him look somewhat less than princely. Sweat trickled down the back of his neck. He had run all the way and he needed to calm down, to think himself royal. His hand paused for a long time over the bell pull. On the far side of the square a girl was selling apples in two languages, one line of her song in English, the next in French. *Pomme* must mean apple, he thought. He closed his eyes and tried to ignore the itch under Quarmy's powdered white wig. He had never worn one for any length of time before and he hoped this one was free of lice.

I am a prince, he told himself, and tugged hard on the bell pull.

Eventually Jack opened the door. He looked past Cato into the street. 'Where's His Highness then?' he hissed.

'Something happened,' Cato said, stepping inside. 'Don't ask! Aren't you mute? Take my card in. It's all right, Jack, honest. Pretend I'm him.'

Cato handed the card to Jack and stepped inside. He waited in the wood-panelled hall, which had been given a Russian touch (with the addition of some huge stuffed animal heads provided by Ezra Spinoza's brother, who was the best taxidermist in Stepney) and prettified (with a couple of portraits of Bella that Mother Hopkins had had knocked up special) to become the London home of the Countess of Pskoff, while Jack, the mute Cossack, went inside. In a moment he was back with Mother Hopkins, her face set with an emotion Cato pitched between anger and fear. She shut the door behind him.

'Cato! For the angels' sake!' Her voice was low. 'Where is Quarmy?'

'Ma, it was me or nothing! I can't explain now – it's all gone head over heels. I can do this, Mother. I *can*. Watch me.'

Mother Hopkins looked at Cato hard for what seemed like an eternity. He didn't flinch. Indeed, he stood more upright and more determined than he had ever done in his life. He met her stare and didn't look away.

Suddenly Mother Hopkins stepped back and brushed down his coat where the mud had clung to it, then took her hanky from her sleeve, spat on it and rubbed his cheek as if the smut of the Seven Dials court still clung to him.

'You do me proud, little Cato,' she said. Cato smiled. She had not called him that for at least two years – it was at least as long as that since he had been any littler than her.

Jack opened the door to the drawing room and went in, walking just behind Mother Hopkins. She curtsied low to Bella, sitting smart in her countess rig.

Mother Hopkins mumbled something unintelligible to Ekaterina. Cato supposed it was cod Russian. The countess nodded and Mother Hopkins backed out of the room, her skirts rustling. 'Oh and, Masha!' The countess clapped her hands. 'Please to bring some chocolate for our guests.'

Inside there was a roaring fire and the smell of rosemary and lavender. Cato felt as if he had been waiting for this all his life.

'My ladies!' Cato said, bowing low and flourishing Quarmy's best three-cornered hat.

Lady Stapleton was a haze of black taffeta. She looked as if solid cloud of black smoke had descended, and sat perched, so that her skirts were in place, on the edge of the chair at the card table opposite Bella. She had been wearing some kind of gauzy veil, which was pulled back, and the effect was of a floating pink and white face in a sea of black. Cato thought of telling Addy and tried hard not to laugh. *Prince*, he said to himself. *I am a prince. I am a prince.*

He looked to Bella first – no, *Ekaterina*, he told himself – and bowed again.

'Countess!' He kept his voice low and silky. 'I did not expect you to have company.'

Ekaterina smiled. 'Elizabeth – the Lady Stapleton – is as a sister to me.'

Cato kept a straight face even though the Russian accent sounded madder than a box of starlings. He wanted so much to look at Lady Stapleton. Was she impressed? What did she think?

'But our business . . .' Cato said smoothly.

'Do not fret so, my prince,' Ekaterina said.

'Prince?' Lady Stapleton looked up. 'Are you truly a prince, sir?'

'I am Prince Quarmy of Bonny, and I am most charmed.' He bowed. 'But I see from your dress that you are in mourning? I trust your Good Lord has your loved one safely in his care.'

Lady Stapleton gasped. 'You are so well spoken!' she said, surprised, and her voice was the same spoiled-little-girl voice Cato remembered from his time in her household at Greenwich. He kept his face smiling and stayed just far enough away so that she could not suddenly on some whim reach out and pinch him.

'I do so hate the mourning. Did I not say, cousin, I am to be in black for half a year! John said a year but I put my foot down. Can you imagine the summer, the parties and dancing, and I am sat in my weeds like a country widow.' Lady Elizabeth looked at Cato. 'I told John: "Sir John," I said, "half a year in black for your father is all I can suffer. Then at least pearl and lilac and lavender, for I must have some relief." Even the house is all draped in black and the mirrors turned to the wall! It is miserable, quite, quite unutterably miserable!'

'I am most sorry for you, my lady. The custom of mourning here in England seems to be a matter of prohibition in dress above all else,' Cato said. 'Has it been long since your father-in-law passed away?'

Lady Stapleton sighed theatrically. 'Nearly four days! Don't tell a soul about the cards.' She looked at Ekaterina. 'He won't tell, will he?'

Ekaterina laughed a deep un-Bella-like laugh. 'I do not think so. Quarmy, come, you will be joining us perhaps?'

'Please, ladies, no!' Cato moved back. 'Cards are not my strong suit. And I know the Countess Ekaterina of old.' He looked at Lady Stapleton. 'I hope our countess has not been leading you astray with those cards, madam.'

The Lady Elizabeth burst into tinkly aristocratic laughter. Cato sat down, lifting the tails of his princely coat so as not to crease them.

'Perhaps,' he said, looking serious, 'this is not the time. Countess, I need your answer to my proposition in all haste.'

Ekaterina turned to Quarmy and smiled. 'I am sure Lady Elizabeth will not mind listening if you have come to discuss what I think you have come to discuss.'

Cato coughed and blushed. 'I did not realize you would have company. And what I have to say is of a most –' he coughed – 'delicate nature.'

'Ooh, this is too, too, intriguing!' Lady Elizabeth clapped her hands. 'I promise, sir, I will say nothing. And why, if I do, you may tell my husband how I am playing at "Laugh and Lie Down" all the day long when I am supposed to be doing nothing but weeping and wailing at the loss of that curmudgeon who was my father-in-law!'

'I have your word then?' Cato asked. 'This will go no further?'

Ekaterina nodded. Lady Elizabeth put down her cards and leaned forward, wide-eyed.

Cato began. 'Well then, my tale is like this. My father's kingdom lies on the coast of West Africa, the Bight of Bonny, where many a ship runs into trouble. You have heard, I expect, of the Bight of Benin?'

The ladies nodded.

Cato waited for a few moments until the room was quiet. The only sound was the crackling of the fire in the grate and the rushing of the wind down the chimney. He leaned close and intoned in a slow, deep voice. '*Beware, all you sailors, the Bight of Benin. Few come out, though many go in!*' Cato paused and took a deep breath before he went on: 'Well, Bonny is worse. Much worse.'

Ekaterina gasped, almost a little too theatrically, Cato thought.

He continued, 'True, some ships are broken, snapped like matchwood on the rocks, but there is another peril, a peril that causes more misery for the Europeans than the rocks of Benin ever do!'

Lady Stapleton sighed. 'My father, Captain Walker – you may have heard of him – indeed, he sailed the African coast many times. He told me so many tales of wrecks and misfortune that they leave me quite cold.' She turned to Ekaterina. 'Shall I lay out the cards, cousin?'

Cato shifted in his seat. It was clearly time to move the tale along. 'This is not a wreck, not quite, for the ship I speak of is, in fact, quite whole.'

'Oh?' Lady Stapleton was dealing cards and didn't look up.

'It was – *is* – her cargo that is of interest.' Cato looked from the countess to Lady Stapleton. 'Some rubies, jade from the east. Bullion stolen from Portuguese privateers in the South China Seas.' Lady Elizabeth took no notice. 'And bolts of the finest Indian silks; yards of sateen woven with gold from China, from the ports of Macau and Cochin, en route to the warehouses of Amsterdam. But sadly, their journey fatefully interrupted.'

Lady Elizabeth stopped dealing. 'Silks?' The look on her face told Cato this would be easy enough.

'I have the inventory here.' He took out a letter from his coat pocket. Aged and sealed and smelling of Africa, it listed satins and taffetas and silks and uncut gems. Stolen gold and more besides. The Lady Elizabeth's eyes grew wide just looking at it.

'And such colours!' Cato said. 'Emeralds and reds, a violet so dazzling my father says it looks like nothing but the sky just before sunset, transformed into cloth. They are of a kind as yet unseen in Europe.'

'But these fabrics, aren't they damaged by the water in the shipwreck? And anyway, won't the owners want them back? That is what happens in these cases, sir, isn't it?' asked Lady Stapleton.

'Ah, no, you see, the misfortune that causes such loss of life is not shipwreck, it is the malaria, the marsh fever. I believe you Europeans are less hardy and not immune to it as we are. The entire crew perished. But the ship, as you may have seen, madam –' here he handed a copy of the *London Gazette* over to Lady Elizabeth – 'is registered lost. They believe it was wrecked. Gone and sunk at the bottom of the Atlantic. The insurers will be reimbursing all the owners. Only my father, his people and ourselves in this room know the truth. So now the ship is his.'

'Only us three in the whole of the world know this truth? That is indeed amazink!' the countess said.

'So what will happen to the silks? Your father will have fine dresses made for his hundreds of savage wives and dress them as if they are Parisiennes!' Lady Elizabeth laughed. The countess joined in and flashed a subtle but cutting look to Cato, which he knew meant *join in*.

Cato felt for the prince. He imagined if he was a prince with a father who was a king, he would look hurt. So he did. 'I can assure you, my father has but two wives, madam.'

At that comment the vaguest look of anxiety passed across the countess's face, and she changed the subject. 'But the cloth, dear prince. You vill bring it here, to London?'

'Well, this is a long and moving story, madam. My father is a king.'

'Yes, yes, and I am the Marchioness of Byfield, we know that!' said Lady Stapleton.

'But he is dependent on the traders for money. Oh, he has land. The Kingdom of Bonny is larger than England.'

'Oh, I do not think that can be possible . . .' She shook her head.

Cato ignored her. 'But our country is not rich. And this opportunity has fallen as if from heaven into our laps. A ship loaded down with expensive cargo. If I can find an investor who will finance a crew, we can change the ship's name and bring the goods to market as our own. Countess, you have been a friend to our family. You could be more of a friend to us now – and, by the by, enrich yourself and have the most beautiful and indeed the most original dresses for the coming season.'

Lady Elizabeth turned the cards over in her hands. The countess looked thoughtful.

'I vill have to be thinking on it. It vould be a most considerable investment,' she replied.

'It would, that is no lie. But there is opportunity for a great return – the cargo speaks for itself. It would be worth more than seven thousand on sale, here in the richest city of all, London!'

'But the risk! Vot if the *Favourite* is recognized? That could happen, could it not? I vould have paid out – how much did you say?'

'I hadn't yet. But the *Favourite*'s home port is Amsterdam. If she has a new name, it's a long shot she'll be remembered.'

The countess paused, eyeing Lady Elizabeth for a reaction. 'So then, Master Prince – how much?' she asked.

Lady Stapleton put the cards aside and stared at Cato in anticipation.

For a second Cato remembered the conversation in The Vipers. Mother Hopkins had said three thousand pounds would be enough for a good house and a decent living. But this was so *easy*. He looked at the Lady Elizabeth, who was fairly drooling at the thought of satins and silks and who must now have a fortune equal to royalty. He took a deep breath.

'Five thousand pounds. Surely a trifle for one such as yourself, Countess.'

The countess looked shocked, and Cato shut his eyes and looked away. Lady Elizabeth had seen the shock too.

'Five thousand pounds?' The countess had her hand to her throat and she talked low. She was looking daggers at Cato, who tried not to squirm. The wood in the fireplace crackled and spat in the silence. Cato crossed his fingers and prayed that no one could see. Perhaps he had gone too far; perhaps he had ruined the lay good and proper.

Lady Elizabeth put down the cards. 'Is that all?'

Cato and the countess turned to look at her.

'You could engage a crew and bring the ship to London for that? I would expect ownership of the cloth and whatever bullion is on board as well as the ship itself.'

Cato and Bella exchanged a quick glance, and Cato hoped his delight was not too obvious. If they pulled this off, then he would be in favour with Mother for ever.

'You vould spare a gown for me, dear cousin?' the countess asked.

'Of course,' Lady Elizabeth said. 'If what you say is true.'

'I have no reason to doubt the prince, sister. His family is well known to me.'

'But what about your husband?' Cato asked. 'He will need to be consulted, no? This is a major investment.'

Lady Elizabeth winked. 'It can be our secret. Ships take an age to get from one side of the world to another! By the time the ship is in London and our dresses made – which will be the most fabulous creations in the city—'

'Indeed, madam, you shall look like birds of paradise! Human angels!' Cato said.

'Yes, yes, heads will turn and we will be most admired. My husband need never know until I have the cargo stored and housed and have made a return.'

'A good return,' Cato added.

'Yes indeed, a very good return.'

'He is bound to be most pleased with his marchioness!' Bella emphasized the point in her best Russian English.

At that moment Mother Hopkins bustled in with the hot chocolate and Cato almost drank the sweet smooth liquid down in one, it tasted so good.

'Saints strike me dumb, Cato Hopkins!' Bella was standing by the fire in the upstairs room at The Vipers, tying her hair up in rags to make it curl. Her face was scrubbed of make-up now, and she was in her nightdress and wrapped in a shawl. She was smiling. 'I thought for a good minute your brains had turned to soup! Five thousand he asked for, Ma!'

Out on the street the watchman called the hour and the church bell at St Andrew's Holborn rang for ten o'clock. Sam was mending a buttonhole on his coat and Jack was polishing his Russian boots. Quarmy sat furthest from the fire; he'd not spoken a word.

Cato had tried to cheer him up since this afternoon, but if anything the good news had made him worse.

'Five thousand pounds! That's two houses and a pair of the finest black Arabians and a flashy four-wheeler!' Jack said, eyes gleaming. 'And some of these Russki boots for you and me, Sam.'

'Now look what you done,' Bella said.

'It just came out!' Cato said. 'It seemed a way to make the trap sweeter.' He stretched out in front of the fire. It had been a good day.

Bella went on, 'You should have heard her, Ma, Lady Elizabeth. All day, on and on about getting the money together before her old man comes home. We went and had the necklace valued – remember, that diamond one she wore to the Ice Ball?'

'Very nice. How much?' Mother Hopkins filled up her pipe.

'One thousand five hundred pounds!' Bella exclaimed. 'The jeweller fairly died and went to heaven just looking at it!'

'Still leaves near on four thousand,' Mother Hopkins said.

'Yeah, well, I reckon as Countess of Pskoff I could always help out with the odd grand. It'd be more of a convincer if she thinks I'm shelling out too. And it's not all roses . . . We went to her private bank, and the manager is a mate of her father's. We're gonna need that ship's inventory for him to look over. He's not happy with her taking so much money out at once. You sure it looks the business?'

Mother Hopkins nodded. 'Right as the Archbishop of Canterbury himself.'

'I never thought I'd say it but, Cato, you're a marvel, a real honest marvel!'

Mother Hopkins lit her pipe. 'Don't get too happy until the money's in our hands, Bella. It's not over yet. When's she paying up?'

'We'll have the necklace tomorrow, to show willing,' Bella said.

'Sam, you take it up to Solomon the Dutchman, over Saffron Hill, get him to make us a copy so good you can't tell one from t'other. And tell him we wants it done by yesterday!'

'And, Ma, the marquess's back from the country next Monday and we need to get the rest of the cash before he can change her mind,' said Bella, warming her hands near the fire.

'And with plenty of luck and hard graft,' Mother Hopkins said, 'not forgetting God's will, we'll be off on the Bath Road by Tuesday morning, chickens!'

12. Reversals of Fortune

IT WAS a beautiful Friday morning. Cato was pleased to be out instead of shut up at The Vipers having to look at Quarmy, whose face registered so low a depression even Bella had commented on it. Mother Hopkins had offered him Sam's bed until Monday and then he would have to sort himself out. Cato felt a little sorry for him but no more. He could work a passage back to Africa, although Cato had heard that a sailor's life was hardly removed from that of a slave. Even Quarmy's title could not protect him from that.

Cato looked up. The sun shone hard and the silver frost glistened and made the city into a fairyland, a magician's palace of church spires, fine townhouses and shining roofs. Cato felt a tug at his heart at the thought of losing all this – there were only a few days until they would be packing up and leaving for Bath. He tried to imagine a life somewhere other than The Vipers but he couldn't. Of course, there'd been times away when he was young and played the slave boy. But one of the things that had been most comforting during the long nights in other people's houses, curled up in a lumpy box bed (if he was lucky; if he was unlucky, on a hard stone kitchen floor), was the thought of coming home. There was nothing to beat coming back into London, cresting Highgate Hill and seeing the city spread out before him like a panorama come to life.

Cato walked out towards Covent Garden and made certain to take in every last detail: the shop signs offering knives and blades, or gloves and trimmings, stays and petticoats, stationery and pens. He thought he'd take a long walk through the market, then back along the Strand and over to St Paul's Churchyard to look at the bookshops, and then perhaps he could walk to the docks by the Tower. He was not needed today, after all. The necklace had been handed over, and all that was left was for Bella to play the countess a little longer and for the documents (forged expertly by another of Mother Hopkins's oldest colleagues) to be signed over and the cash exchanged. Cato knew better than to walk too far up west and be seen, but today was the first day the weather had allowed a walk for pleasure. He sighed out loud, and a cloud of white smoke left his mouth and drifted up into the air. Surely Bath would never measure up to London in any shape or form.

Cato reminded himself not to make his feelings known. Addy would be back soon and she was bound to moan about Bath enough for both of them. She hadn't been born here and yet she loved it just as much as he did.

'Cato?' He was walking in between the costers' donkey carts clustered around the Russell Street side of the market when he thought he heard Addy's voice shouting at him.

'Cato!' He stopped and looked round, and there she was. She was leaning against a grimy stone pillar of the market colonnade, out of breath and red in the face from a long run.

'Addeline?' He couldn't help smiling. 'I was thinking of you! Only this very instant! This world is always stranger than any ballad!' He hugged her straight away without thinking. But Addy pulled back and Cato could see she was shaking.

'What is it?'

'Oh, thank goodness! You've saved me a trip to The Vipers!'

Addy was wearing her housemaid's dress with an extra shawl tied round her top half and over her head. She looked like any costermonger's daughter, only one that had seen less of the sun.

'Cato, I only have a moment. I'm supposed to be in Golden Square buying needles. Please! Just let me speak!'

'Are you all right?' he asked, worried now.

'Listen! Get back to The Vipers now and tell Bella to get herself all Russianed up and go and sit in Soho looking the lady!'

'What?'

'Cato! Shush up! The marquess rode home with the devil on his tail this morning. He's come from the country a pauper, so he says.' Cato tried to speak but Addy went on, 'He's grunting and snapping like a badger that's had its rear end nailed to the floor before they let the rats on it. He was so mad he smashed the Chinese vases in the hall – them ones that're bigger than me – with his riding crop! Once he finds out what his missus has done with those sparklers, we are done for!'

Cato said nothing and looked at her. 'I don't understand . . .'

'He's bellowing about the debts he's been left to deal with, an' shouting as they'll have to sell everything, Cato, *everything*! Tell Ma to get everything packed up – we might have to make a run for it tonight.'

'It can't be that bad, surely,' Cato said. Even though he'd seen – with his own eyes – all the assets the Stapletons owned, he still felt a twisting in his guts, as if he might be sick. He shook the feeling away. What Addy said could not be true.

'A pauper overnight? I don't believe it. He's making a sit-down meal of a starling.'

'We've been let go, Cato! The whole household, as of tomorrow, every one of us laid off except the lady's maid and the master's valet, given our leave and told to make the best of it. Right now, back at St James's, he's making an inventory of the carpets and silver plate! He's not fooling!'

Cato tried to think. 'You must have the wrong end of the stick, Addy—'

'No! I know what I seen. Now just do as I say. You ain't seen the master when he's angry. He may be a Member of Parliament but he acts like any other buck in a rage when he's in his cups. He's already downed a bottle of port this morning.'

The church clock rang for a quarter to eleven.

'I must return. The cook will miss me, even if the Stapletons won't. Go on, go! Quickly! Tell them to get over to Carfax with Bella wearing something that will make the marquess forget!'

Cato was hiding in the upstairs rooms at Carfax in his princely coat when the new marquess arrived in a flashy two-seater. Looking out through a crack in the shutters, he saw there was no footman, only a driver, and when he got down from the coach, the marquess slammed the door so hard Cato imagined it would come off.

The marquess had walked up to the front door before he remembered his wife, who was obviously not used to getting herself out of a carriage, and had waited immobile for someone to open her door. The marquess bellowed in the direction of the coach so loud the horses jumped.

'Come on, woman!'

Cato could see that something had happened to change him. He looked totally different from the time he had seen him at the Ice Ball. He seemed to have aged at least ten years, and the dark circles under his eyes – the result of his overnight ride from the country – made him look closer to a kind of monster than a young nobleman with a beautiful wife and a house in the finest part of town.

The whole square watched as the Lady Elizabeth clambered down, almost falling over and practically in tears. Cato could read off her face that everything Addy had said was true. They had lost everything.

Cato listened as Jack was pushed aside and – supposedly being mute – could say nothing.

'Where is she? Where is the Russian trollop who has bewitched my wife?' The marquess bellowed louder than the boys who cried the news at Fleet Street.

Jack opened the door to the drawing room, to reveal Bella, or rather the Countess of Pskoff, and Mother Hopkins, done up as her retainer, Masha.

Cato just managed to hear the countess welcome the Stapletons in an accent familiar to lovers of caviar and wild bears, when the drawing-room door was shut. This was followed by shouting, although he could not make out any words, only that it was deep-voiced shouting.

He crept down the stairs, even though Jack tried to shoo him back up.

'Wait until you're sent for!' Jack hissed.

'I need to listen!' Cato whispered. 'I need to know how Bella is playing him.'

Jack stood aside. 'Indeed, you're right.'

Cato crept up to the drawing room and stood with his ear to the wooden door. The countess's voice was smoother than honey and Cato marvelled at Bella's capacity to keep a cool head and prevent her accent from slipping.

'You are a marquess now, sir?' she enquired.

'For all the bloody good it'll do me!' He was still shouting. 'We are ruined! Ruined by my profligate father, who preferred the cards and the horses and the lowest sort of women to any kind of prudence! And then ... and then my ... my *wife* –' he spat the word out like the worst oath imaginable – 'tells me she's only gone and handed the best of the family jewels over to some darkie prince! As if such a thing exists.'

'I can be assurink you, sir, the Prince of Bonny is a most honourable and trustworthy young man. I vould be trustink him vith my life.'

'Yes, John, he is.' Lady Elizabeth's voice was high and tremulous.

'And I think –' the countess was speaking again – 'if you can, perhaps, calm yourself – take this wodka – he may even be offerink you a way out of penury and back to the fortune which you and your lovely wife indeed deserve . . .'

As the countess spun out the scheme, she explained that the prince did not realize the true value of the cargo, and that the return of their investment would be threefold. What's more, the investors would be left master of a sea-going ship. She had investigated the *Favourite*, the countess said, and they would be able to sell it on in London or Bristol for a few thousand. Failing that, they could lease it to merchant venturers, and make a decent income, far above and beyond the five thousand the Prince of Bonny had requested.

'It is, like ze ship itself, a watertight investment,' the countess said, and laughed at her own joke. 'And there is no problem, my lord, no one forces you to make money. I can only put my hand on two thousand pounds here in London, but you may have your pretty necklace back and use it to pay off all your many creditors. I vill send my man round to fetch the prince here in person, and he can return your necklace. Even though it may take a day or two, I can find another investor to take your place – someone who has enough, how you say in English, cash . . . ?'

Cato closed his eyes. Bella had gone too far. Never insult your mark. He could only hear a growling sort of noise from Stapleton and his wife's high-pitched twittering about opportunity.

'But the African, won't he be expecting the ship back?' the marquess asked.

The countess laughed her tinkly Russian laugh before she spoke. 'And how will he get it back, hmm? Rowink some kind of raft up ze Thames? I think not. Our gain is his loss. And as I said, we are all so much more deservink . . .'

Cato knocked at Carfax a half-hour later and Jack let him in. He had a soft leather bag with the copy of the necklace Mother Hopkins had rustled up from the diamond dealer in Saffron Hill. It had cost her the last of their savings but it looked good, although he'd been warned to be careful with it because if it fell hard on to stone, the paste gems were sure to shatter.

Jack showed him in. The new Marquess of Byfield was calmer, but he still looked grim. His wife was all nerves, hands fluttering from her throat to her face, shifting in her chair so the fabric of her black mourning dress rustled.

Cato bowed. 'Ladies and gentlemen, I am Quarmy, Prince of Bonny. Countess, your man informs me there is a problem.'

'I'd have thought he couldn't inform a cockerel to crow seeing as how the brute cannot speak,' the marquess said.

The countess flashed Cato a look sharper than razors, and he felt his heart speed up so fast he thought it might burst.

'Your note, madam,' he said at last, and flourished a piece of paper from his pocket. 'I brought the jewels, and though it pains me to return them to their beautiful owner –' he smiled at Lady Elizabeth – 'I am sure they will look a thousand times better on you.'

The marquess scowled, but Cato smiled on. Bella was playing it light, as if she didn't care, and he should follow her lead.

'My good friends wish to withdraw from our scheme, Prince,' said the countess.

'I am most sorry to hear this but, as they say on the coast of Bonny –' Cato paused here as if translating African to English – '*What is to is, must is . . .*' He nodded sagely. He knew this was not an African proverb, but one he had heard an elderly Jamaican prize fighter who frequented

The Vipers use more than once. He went on, 'I had already sent word by ship home to my father, and you were also lucky. I had found a buyer for the diamonds and was to sell them tomorrow. Ah, well. Countess, you promised me two thousand pounds – I suppose you cannot raise your stake?'

The countess shook her head. 'Alas, no. If only I were at home, it would be done. But I am sure we can find another partner, no?'

Cato allowed himself to look a little troubled. 'Speed, as I said before, is of the essence. I will leave the stones and get to the Royal Exchange at once. Good day!' He left the leather pouch on the card table and bowed again.

'If you are ever in Bonny, my lady . . .' He kissed the countess's hand and left.

If the plan was to work, the marquess's greed should get the better of him. He would call the prince back and offer the entire investment before he reached the street.

Nothing happened. Jack opened the front door and Cato stepped out into the square.

His heart felt empty. They had invested so much time and money into this; they owed so many favours! Cato walked down the steps. They had the diamonds, at least. They would fund a cottage in Bath and he hoped there was call for good locksmiths in the West Country.

Cato turned the corner by the French church into Hog Lane when he heard footsteps closing behind him. He had the prince's fine coat and hat, which would make a guinea or two. He speeded up, but couldn't resist looking round. He relaxed when he saw it was Jack clumping down the street in his boots, red-faced.

Cato looked past him in case he was not alone. 'Jack! Saints preserve us!' he said. 'I thought I was to be skinned!'

Jack came close and leaned against the church railings, doubled up. 'I've been behind you from the square, only I couldn't shout on account of being a bloody mute!' He straightened up, a grin across his face wider than the Thames at Chelsea. 'It's only gone and bloody worked! It's only worked!' He thumped Cato hard on the back. 'The marquess wants to rebuild his fortune. And he's starting with a gold-plated investment in a ship that don't even exist! Come on, I've been sent to bring you back.'

13. Newgate Prison, Dawn, September 1712

I DON'T KNOW how I managed to sleep, hands and feet shackled, but I suppose one can get accustomed to anything. I had thought to stay awake, given that this was to be my last night on this earth. But I had such a good dream. Addeline with her hair wild, laughing and laughing.

Then the Ordinary kicked me in the ribs and now I was sure that I was awake and that it was morning. It wasn't due to the light, but from the sounds of life beyond the prison walls – the handcarts and animals and horse-drawn wagons trundling along the street; not to mention a woman not too far off, inside the walls, sobbing.

I tried to sit upright. 'I am to hang today,' I said aloud, half hoping he would laugh and that this room, this stench, these sounds were the dream.

'Death comes to all of us,' the Ordinary said. 'Please, we have little time. I would have more of your tale so it may be published and quite the talk of the town before you are cut down.'

'Those are hardly words to inspire me, sir,' I said.

'It is only the truth, young man.'

Young man. I would never now be old, I thought. Not see myself with a proper beard or with a son and daughter of my own. I sighed.

'On the subject of my crime I am sworn to silence,' I said, and he kicked me again. It was a small pleasure to have it within my power to cause this human blood-sucker some irritation.

'The diamonds! All London is rife with rumour: where did they go? Off with the Czar of Russia's daughter, it's said.'

'She was a countess, not a princess! Anyway, the truth may be less romantic. Have you never thought, perhaps, that the Stapleton diamonds were never the real thing in the first place?'

He sneered. 'I will play no more games with you, you imp!'

'I will tell you how I was caught, but even then I fear we won't reach the end of my tale,' I said, and the church clock at St Sepulchre's chimed six. 'The cart will come for me at ten.'

In the darkness of the condemned cell I heard the Ordinary sharpen his quill. I took a long breath and began. After all, I had naught else to pass the time, and my family, the friends I once had, were long gone. Living other lives in Bath.

I was already dead to them a long time ago when I was foolish enough to be caught.

So I spoke.

'All had gone to plan – no, scratch that . . . We had, in fact, exceeded all our goals. We had enough rhino to live wherever we pleased. Bella had in mind the dresses she would have made, Jack the pair of Arabians; Sam was planning on a lighter chair design that would make his job a great deal more comfortable. Even Quarmy, our genuine African prince, was smiling occasionally. He had decided to stay in London, and Mother, heart softened by so much goree, had promised to give him a few guineas to set him up as a music master in a charity school. The idea suited him, he said, although in truth I could not see our prince inducing sulky ten-year-olds to scratch out tunes!

'See, we had more than the full five thousand in cash, on top of the diamonds. The carter had been hired, the upstairs rooms at The Vipers cleared, and the party! That Tuesday night all London – well, all London that mattered – was there. Ivan, the cove with the dancing bear (he left the bear at home); Solly the Dutchman; even Master Tunnadine, who had been pressured not to set foot in the capital ever again, had made his way to The Vipers. And, yes – write this down – I witnessed Mother Hopkins shed more than a tear or two.

'All was well and in full swing. Bella had opened the proceedings with her recital of "My Lady's Revenge". I had played and Quarmy was to play too – he was a better player than me – and I planned to ask Addeline to dance. Oh, we had often danced *near* to each other – many times, in fact. But this was to be different. I was going to ask her, the way Sam asked the glove-shop girl, or Jack had once asked Bella, if you get my meaning.

'So I've only been going over and over it in my head all day. How I'll ask her and how she'll answer, and I'm hoping hard she won't just look at me with her dark grey eyes and laugh. And I've been so bound up with that that I don't notice Quarmy's not there. I'm getting myself all twisted up just thinking about it, seeing the picture of it in my head. I had spoken to him earlier and he'd promised to play the tune Addy likes best: "The Thames Flows Sweetly". So I'm pushing through the crowd in the bar at The Vipers, only no one's seen him since dark. I go upstairs, thinking he's having a weep over his lost love, but he's not there. His fine princely coat is hung up on the back of the door but there's no sign of Quarmy.

'Then all sorts of things just go rushing through my head. 'Cause there was always that distance with Quarmy, looking back on it – and I've had more than enough time in here to look back on it. I can see it's more his upbringing than anything else, but I suppose . . . I suppose I was more than a little jealous of the cove. So there's me, reckoning on how maybe he's scarpered with the lot – the money . . . everything – and ready to round up Jack and Sam and scour the city looking for him.

'But they're well into their cups and not ready to move anywhere, and Sam says of course Quarmy's not taken the cash because Ma's hidden it safe, but then Jack asks if I've seen his Bella, which I haven't, since she sang. So then I'm thinking they've only gone and run off together. Addy puts me right. She's sitting nursing her ale in the corner, and I'm wishing I could ask her to dance anyway. I would, excepting it's Daley the locksmith singing "The Girl I Left Behind", which, in case you do not know, is a very mournful tune indeed. Even more so when it is sung by a locksmith who can scarce carry a tune.

'I know why Addy is down: she no more wants to leave town than a cat wants to give up the seat closest to the fire. She sighs and smiles a sad smile, and for an instant I wish that The Vipers was empty except for the two of us.

'"I thought you was after Quarmy?" she says. "Wasn't he going to play? If he isn't, then will you, 'cause I don't reckon I can take much more of Old Man Daley's warbling. And play something jolly to lift the spirits, for Christ's own sake!"

'So I says to her: "I think Quarmy's vanished. Run off with Bella and all our blood and bread. Into the night."

'"You don't mean it?" she says.

'And I just shrugged. "No one else is bothered," I says.

'Old Daley stops singing and there's cheering and applause, and suddenly Mother Hopkins is standing on the bar of The Vipers and the crowd are baying for a song.

'Then I turn to Addy. No chance of a dance but I had a plan. "Let's go and see what's happened," I say, and take her by the hand out into the dark London streets. The cold air stings like a bucket of frozen water. But I can feel Addy's smiling to be out, just from the pressure of her hand in mine, and the spring in her step. I realize Bella's probably off kissing Ivan out of sight of Jack, and Quarmy's probably chasing his sweetheart's shadow. But that doesn't matter. It's me and Addeline. Out in the dark. One last time.

'It was completely black that night, as if London was wearing a cloak of pitch. I remember that well – no moon at all, and as we walked away from the noise and the light of The Vipers, it seemed like the city folded us in, like we were a part of it. Can you imagine that, Sir Ordinary? It makes me fair shiver thinking I'll never know that feeling again.

'Like I said, we was on the way down to Long Acre when a link boy runs towards us out of the blackness, his torch yellow and blinding, lighting the way.

'So Addy shouts, "Oi!"

'"Who's that?" the boy shouts back. "If you want me to take you to Leicester Fields, that'll be tuppence as it's gone midnight!" He is tiny and his voice is high and squeaky.

'"It's Miss Addeline Hopkins, and we only want information," Addy replies.

'"Addeline Hopkins?" He's slightly scared, and Addy is pleased, I can tell.

'"Oi, little 'un! Have you been working the Garden all night?"

'"What if I have?"

'"You haven't seen a young cove, darker than nibs here?" Addeline asks him.

'"Patterns all on his face?" says the boy. Quarmy is hard to miss, as I'm sure you can imagine, sir.'

The Ordinary nodded his head as he wrote.

'So she says: "Yeah, the very one!"'

'"You 'is mates?" the boy asks. "Only he was carted off to the lock-up in St Anne's with some red-headed piece who was swearing like a sailor. Turned the air bluer than my fingers."

'Addy and I looked at each other then. The link boy held out his hand and we did the honest thing by him, then we sped up towards St Anne's. The redhead had to be Bella, who'd taken the precaution of washing her hair with that abominable stuff that smells of nothing but the night-soil cart so she wouldn't be mistaken for Ekaterina.

'"I can spring 'em," I said to Addy.

'"I know," Addeline said, and squeezed my hand. And so we both fair hurtled through the dark to Soho.'

I shifted position and made myself as comfortable as I could. The Ordinary stopped to stretch his hand.

'They were there all right. Quarmy mute and inconsolable even when we turned up and whispered at them though the bars. Bella was with him, and she was fighting off the only other unlucky fool in the lock-up, some young buck with a name I don't remember, drunk as a lord and puking up as if his stomach had no bottom to it.

'Well, when Bella sees me, she knows they're as good as out, so she stops with the yelling and tells Addy to go round the front and get her cards out. She knows as the gaoler likes a game, 'cause she tried to talk him round, but he thought himself too clever to be drawn by a prisoner.

'So I ask Quarmy what happened, and he says: "Bella had walked me to Bedfordbury, to buy a new G-string for my fiddle, when we are accosted. Accosted by a sailing man with a cockaded hat."

'"A captain, Cato," Bella adds. "And, oh, your jaw will drop. Only your friend and mine. Captain Walker of Greenwich."

'Then Quarmy says, "He grabbed me – quite ungentlemanly – tight by the elbow, and then Bella pulled on the other side and I blushed profusely on account of the names he called her."

'"At least he didn't have me down as Russian!" Bella says.

'Quarmy carries on: "He says, the captain says, 'I know those marks. I know them!' in such a tone as to send shivers down your spine."

'I stopped the conversation there on account of it being all the better to talk after they were free – if I had but known then that the day would never come ...' I sighed and pulled off some biting insect – a louse, most likely, but I must admit I was grateful the cell was still quite dark so as I couldn't see it and count its infernal legs.

'Go on, man!' said the Ordinary. 'Time is running and passing – all Newgate will be up and we all have our allotted tasks and time. So, you're saying Captain Walker, he thought Quarmy was you?'

'Well, in a manner of speaking,' I said. 'He thought Quarmy was the cove what had swindled his son-in-law. See, Captain Walker had sailed up and down the West Coast of Africa more times than most. He'd seen markings like Quarmy's before; he knew he was royalty – could tell he was the real thing, and he'd been on the lookout for an African ever since his daughter had confided to her mother that all was well and their fortune would soon be restored by a prince from Africa.' I smiled to myself. 'I'd have loved to have been a mouse in their skirting board! I can see it all: "Mama, Mama, this nice African prince has gone and sold us a ship and its cargo. Knock-down price! The money we'll make! Maybe Papa can captain the boat?"

'Thing we didn't reckon on was that old Captain Walker knows Bonny well. We never knew this particular nugget of information. He knows the tale's a fishy one and he works out the diamonds are cockerels' eggs and as far from being the real thing as day is from night. He knows now that his daughter has been swindled rotten and is not about to let it lie.'

I leaned back against the cold cell wall. Someone was awake and singing a hymn, asking God to save his soul. The Ordinary must have been listening too because he went and said that was one tune I ought to be practising myself to sing as I danced the hangman's jig. I said nothing. I wanted my last dance to have been with Addeline.

'So did you spring them, your associates?' the Ordinary asked.

'Is the Queen a lady?' I replied.

Outside, the sky was getting lighter. Through the barred window the sky had a blush of light that turned it brown. The city was almost completely awake. I imagined the carter brushing down his horse, the one that would pull the cart with me and my fellow unfortunates to the edge of town, where the Oxford Road gives way to fields. Where the famous, possibly world-famous, triple tree would hang three of us at once and give the crowd – for there was sure to be a good crowd – a free day's entertainment.

A rat crawled under the Ordinary's chair, a fat one that had lost the better part of its tail. The sight of it caused my mouth to water and I felt that ashamed I shut my eyes and turned away.

What had I become in here? No wonder Mother Hopkins did her damnedest never to see inside these walls ever again. No wonder that, rather than fight for me, they left and ran away to their new lives in the west.

'Is that a tear, boy?' the Ordinary said. 'Are you ready to confess and save your poor benighted soul?'

'It's not tears, just a piece of straw.' I rubbed my eyes. I thought again of the ride in the cart to my end, and suddenly I remembered one last thing. I knew she'd never know, but I bet she'd read the news sheets, if they had 'em in Bath. I wanted Addy to be proud of me.

I sat up. 'There'll be no confession, either. I never brought shame to no one,' I said.

The Ordinary looked at me, and in the dim light I saw myself through his eyes. Dirty, shabby . . . if I was to be hanged, I should at least go out looking better than a boy who had rolled in dirt his whole life. I thought of the cutpurse's embroidered jacket at the Frost Fair, or Quarmy's good princely one.

'If I tell you how I was taken—'

'The diamonds, that'll be the clincher,' the Ordinary said, eyes shining.

'If you get me a good coat and hat to wear, I'll whisper in your ear what happened just before I'm wedded to the noose. It'll look like a confession but I'll make you a wealthy man, and no mistake.'

The Ordinary shifted in his seat and I knew I almost had him.

'I know you!' he said. 'You're slippery as a Thames eel. You might change your mind, and the money I get from the last words is for burial. I can't be paid twice.'

'No, man!' I said, for the idea was running away in my head. 'I don't care about my burial – the surgeons may have me and turn me inside out for all I care. I've no doubt there'll be plenty of interest in a Negro. Think about that.' I said the words like a brave man and told myself I would be in no position to care if I was cut open or my innards used as bunting in the surgeons' hall. I wasn't going to show fear to this man, nor to anyone. I knew to keep it all inside.

The Ordinary thought for a while, then put out his hand for me to shake.

'It better be the best coat in Cheapside!' I said.

The Ordinary was smiling wide and showed his yellow teeth, which matched the London sky. I could tell he was imagining the diamonds in his pocket. He was thinking about never having to work in the hovel that was Newgate ever again. 'Done!' he said.

I sat back. I hid my smile. It was just like old times.

'So, where was we?' he said, picking up his quill. 'Oh yes, the lock-up in Soho. You spring the redhead and the prince, and then what?'

'Well, what happened was that it didn't quite go to plan – I'd be a free man if it had! The drunk had taken a shine to Bella and stumbled after her through the door, yelling, "Love and freedom! My flame-haired Venus!"

'The gaoler realized he'd been played for a mug, blew his whistle and grabbed Addy, guessing rightly she'd been distracting him with the cards. She wriggled and stamped hard on his foot but he wouldn't let her go, so I pulled her off him. She runs like the blazes and I was ready to follow, but Bella's new boyfriend goes to throw a punch at the gaoler, misses and knocks me clean out. It must have looked like one of the plays at Bartholomew Fair. A ripe comedy.' I shook my head, remembering. 'I was that close to getting away.'

'A *tragedy* for you, young man!' The Ordinary laughed at his own joke, which I thought particularly poor.

'So when I woke, I was here. Not *here* exactly – not the condemned cell. Just in with the usual cream of London society you have lodging here. My head throbbed and my throat was sore from thirst. I must have been out cold for days.'

'Pah! I heard it was from night to noon. The gaoler at St Anne's said you'd opened the locks by magic. He said you weren't human. It was the start of the rumours. Wanted you out of his lock-up sharpish,' the Ordinary said.

'That was the end of my luck,' I said, and sighed. 'Captain Walker had his daughter identify me as the prince and he smiled like a pig in clover when the beak put on his black cap and pronounced my death.'

'Well, boy! You should have pointed out the money! For that fortune – all those pounds and the real diamonds, the real Stapleton sparklers – they must be somewhere.'

I sighed again. 'I am in Newgate. I am a walking dead man. Wealth will not spring me now,' I said.

'But you managed to get out of Newgate, and the warder, Mr Gittens, said it were impossible!' The parson came close and I could smell the beer on his breath. 'How did you do it? Mr Gittens told me one night he thought you must have a kind of philtre, a potion to make yourself invisible. But I told him, I says: "The boy's as black as night.

He'll just keep his eyes and mouth shut and no one'll be any better at knowing his whereabouts!"' The Ordinary laughed so hard he almost fell off his stool.

'Your wit knows no bounds, sir,' I said, and the old fool believed me.

I waited until he had quite finished his hysteria and kept my voice low. 'If I tell you how it was done,' I said, 'could you see your way to sending out for a good linen shirt? One of the ones with plenty of cloth in the sleeves?'

The Ordinary coughed. 'Maybe, but that'll be the last of it. Coats! Shirts! It'll be shammy britches next! I'm not made of the rhino!' He calmed down and looked at me. 'So, how was it done then? My pen is ready.'

'No invisibility potions or magics, I'm afraid. I would that it were all magic and you would blink and I'd be gone, into the west with the old heroes.' I closed my eyes for a moment. 'It was all a matter of practicalities, but, I warrant, well done and a good tale.'

'Well, get on and tell it then, boy. Time is our master!'

'The shirt?'

'I gave you my word.'

I tried to study the man's face the way Mother Hopkins had taught me. Did the cove hold my gaze? Yes, but the cast of his eye was distinctly dull, and from the softness around the Ordinary's mouth I reckoned he was greedy enough for the rhino that he'd fetch me the clothes and then sell the pieces on afterwards to gallows gawpers for tuppence a piece.

I went on, 'So, as I said, when I came into Newgate, they placed me in the Master's Yard. There were thirty of us packed in and I knew there'd be no chance of delivery from there so I made a fuss, a ruckus – staged a fight with Blueskin Doherty.'

'I remember that!'

'And so I was moved. To the rooms called the Stone Castle. Although it was neither entirely stone nor in any shape or form a castle.'

'We used it as the chapel once,' said the parson.

'Yes, a few old chairs and a rather large hole in the ceiling, as I recall.'

'You lie! There is no hole in the roof there!' he exclaimed.

'I went through it! Up through the chimney breast and out on to the roof. I've always been what you might call flexible. And I'd done it once before when I was younger, stuck in a fine house with Mother Hopkins calling to me to get out quick and no other way. And that's how I did it. I caught a good fine rat for Margaret Vernon, that girl who was in for nailing fine French-woven ladies' manteaus to shop fronts. She will look the other way if you can give her anything of value. She was in the Press Yard, outside the Stone Castle, and she heard the noise I was making and kindly sang "The Dublin Girls' Farewell" as loud as she could while I knocked a few of the bricks away and climbed and climbed.'

'God's teeth, boy, the chimney! Wasn't it close as hell in there?' said the Ordinary.

'Perhaps,' I said. 'But when you can see freedom winking at you in a square of moonlight, it's funny how's you'll put up with a deal of discomfort.'

The Ordinary shook his head and whistled, and I could see his brow furrowing with the effort of imagining wanting to be free so badly that there was close to nothing you wouldn't do . . .

'Be sure, sir,' I said, 'that I'd be out again if I didn't have these damned chains. You wouldn't see me for dust . . .' And in my mind's eye I pictured the road to Bath. Me following the cart, watching Addeline swing her legs off the back and listening to Bella and Jack falling out and making up ten times before we even crossed Hounslow Heath.

'I was only caught,' I said, remembering, 'when the alderman – the one in for embezzlement – saw me as I jumped down on to the roof of the warder's office and swore blind he'd seen Satan leaping out of the hearts of men and on to the warder's quarters. Margaret tried her hardest to dissuade him, but he stared until he realized it was not Satan but merely a boy, and a boy escaping at that. It was him what gave the alarm, and he kept up his noise even after Margaret walloped him with the pot of ease – which, she told me, had recently been filled brimful.'

'Aye.' The Ordinary laughed. 'The man smelled for weeks. But he was let off with transportation for giving you up. And you merely leaped up the chimney! I think the invisibility potion makes a better tale, and if you are willing, I may embroider your tale all the better to sell a few. My daughter wishes a wedding next Michaelmas and we will need every coin I can make. At least that won't be a trouble to you; the future is a terrible thing.'

I think to myself that I would dearly love any kind of future. Long ago, on the outside, I had thought transportation worse than death, no life better than a life of slavery. I shut my eyes. I would give anything for a chance of life now; grab any opportunity to keep my heart beating and the blood running safe within my veins and not left to drain away on the surgeon's slab.

The prison is awake now. The Ordinary gets up and stretches, picks up his stool in one hand and bids me farewell.

'I'll fetch the best coat I can, boy.' He leans close. 'And don't forget. I want the news of the diamonds before you drop. I'll make sure the executioner sends you off sharp and snaps your neck before the pain takes hold, boy, and that's the truth. If not, you'll take your time, and your last dance may be a deal more painful and last much too long for your liking.'

I nod. I can say nothing for fear my voice will be no more than a squeak. I must stay strong. This day will see my last act, and I will go out like a man.

14. The Road to the West

THE ORDINARY keeps his word, and when I step, blinking, out into the grey morning light of the prison yard, I am at least clad like the gentleman I will never now be. The coat is dark blue, with embroidery of silver and grey. It reminds me of the River Thames at night. The shirt is soft linen and, although I can tell it is not brand new from the worn softness of the cloth, it is white and the cuffs are well-fashioned lace.

The others in the cart with me are French Peter Villeneuve of Spitalfields, who stole two bolts of cloth and coshed a watchman, then most viciously slandered the judge, and Mary Cut and Come Again, who said she fenced the Duke of Marlborough's silver but I reckon as she made that up. I had heard her name before and knew she was no more than a pickpocket, but a good one for all that.

They had taken the shackles off my feet in the condemned cell, and I was unsteady, as it had been weeks since I had been free to walk around. My hands, though, were again chained.

'Poor Cato,' French Peter says, helping me stand. 'They treat you miserably. Where we are bound it can't be any worse.' He calls the chief turnkey over. 'Sir. Most gentlemanly warder, will you not loose the boy's hands of these damned knuckle-confounders on this, our last journey?'

The turnkey wobbles across the yard. He is huge, no doubt from all the food that was delivered to the prison for us inmates but got no farther than his own table.

'We've orders not to. The lad's like quicksilver and we do not trust him not to vanish between here and Tyburn.'

'Have a heart!' Mary says, and I blush at her concern. 'Sir, will you not look at the boy! His legs have forgotten how to hold him up – he can barely walk, let alone run!'

'Them's the orders!' says the turnkey, and he opens the massive dark gates of Newgate. I see the street and the city for the first time in months, and in truth my heart leaps and I find it hard to contain the joy in my heart as the cart rattles and sways out into Snow Hill. I smell the meat market at Smithfield and hear the sound of the cattle penned and waiting; waiting for the same fate as I am to face soon enough.

As we cross the stinking Fleet river (which to my nose smells sweeter than any violets), I see two ladies on the Holborn Road, and my heart leaps higher still for I am sure the fairer one is Bella. But as we get closer, I realize they are only acquaintances of French Peter, and not known to me at all. They call out and rush to the cart and throw their arms round his neck and kiss him as the cart trundles slowly west.

And I am sad again, knowing my family will not be there to call out to me or blow me kisses. I try and tell myself that Mother Hopkins was only ever Mother in name, but in my heart I know that isn't true. However hard I curse her for my situation, I know she cared more than many flesh-and-blood mothers.

The crowd grows thicker up to St Giles, and then there are faces in the crowd I know of old from the print shops, and even Daley the locksmith's boy. I don't recognize him at first, for he has grown a foot in the months I have been locked away. But he calls my name: 'Cato! Cato Hopkins!' and seems exceedingly pleased to see me.

I shout back, 'I cannot wave, young Daley.'

He draws near and leans close. 'My father bids you adieu,' he says aloud, then whispers soft so none but I can hear, 'And your mother sends you this to see you on your way to a much better place.' Then he kisses me on the cheek – I am so surprised I would have jumped; then I feel something in the cuff of my coat – something hard and metal – and I know instantly what it is. A pick. One of Daley's best, no doubt.

I could swear the sun, at that moment, strained harder to shine behind the iron-grey curtain of cloud. Perhaps I am not yet quite forgotten.

I shake the pick out of my cuff and into my hand. I sit hard against the side of the cart so my hands will not be seen and begin my work. The thought of hands free to move is more than bliss eternal.

We turn into the Oxford Road and the crowd are now three abreast. As the cart goes, so the mob follows. Mary Cut and Come Again waves like the Queen on her way to open Parliament, and French Peter stands up and begins blowing kisses. He has many admirers and, from the cries of the penny-sheet sellers, many stories. But there are many that cry for me too, and my spirits rise a little, listening.

'The boy who escaped! The boy who nearly got away! The boy who stole the Stapleton diamonds!'

I smile, and since I can neither stand nor wave, incline my head in recognition. For seconds – no, minutes – the thought that in an hour I will be dead is forgotten. We are like minor royalty, or some out-of-town nabobs, feted by the crowd, whistled at and called out to. French Peter is now leaning from the cart and kissing every girl who offers her cheek or lips. Several swoon as if he is some kind of prince. If only Quarmy was here to see it.

Some point at me and smile, and nod, and ask if I may touch their child's withered arm. Eventually the crowd is so dense the cart practically stops until some of the magistrate's men that walk alongside are forced to push the people out of the way.

Then, from above the noise of the crowd, I hear the sound of a fiddler, playing a tune I know well.

I find myself mouthing the words of 'The Thames Flows Sweetly', and before the last line my hands are free, the shackles bumping along empty on the floor of the cart. I stretch and bend them behind my back, at first worried the magistrate's men might see, but they are too busy gawping at the ankles of French Peter's admirers. I stretch my arms out in front of me, below the level of the sides of the cart, feeling the relief in my shoulders. Mary Cut and Come Again sees and smiles, but says nothing.

I push myself up to see if I can spot the fiddler, and, no lie, it is Quarmy! He is there, in the throng at Oxford Market, and he bows low at me and smiles. Even though there were times when I cursed him in prison for being our downfall, I cannot help but smile back. Two faces I know! In such a short space of time! Maybe if Quarmy comes close, I can ask him to send a message to Addeline and the others – maybe a last word or two. Perhaps he has some news, some hope.

'Quarmy!' I shout and wave. Then again, louder, 'Quarmy!' He plays on. I am yelling and waving my enfeebled arms. Perhaps he can do something: make a diversion, overturn the cart. Perhaps Mother is in disguise – is she the woman

I can see selling watercress? 'Oi! Mother, Mother!' I shout. The woman turns to face me and it is not her. A wave of anger breaks behind my eyes. My teeth hurt, my hands are both in fists. Quarmy is not looking at me; he cares only for himself, head bent over his fiddle, playing a sweet tune, while I am on my way to go to heaven on a string. I curse and spit. Mary puts an arm round me, but I push her away. I wipe my face and it is damp. The anger turning to tears, I breathe deeply. I will not cry.

The Ordinary, riding along on a fat grey mare, sees my hands are free, but Mary puts a finger to her lips and I, now calmer, mouth the word *Diamonds* slowly and clearly, and he looks straight ahead. I keep my eyes on Quarmy, even as the cart moves away. But the tune fades and so does he.

I am, once more, alone in the crowd.

As we near Tyburn, I can almost smell the open space that lies to the west. It is the end of London, and the end of me. The spring has been late coming and now it is autumn again. Mother Hopkins would be making apple and blackberry comfits and pies. I wonder if she had found her house in Bath. I wonder if Sam and Jack and Bella and

Addeline are sitting around a polished wooden table, laughing and joking and not thinking one jot of me.

A drummer beats out a death tattoo. Now I can see the triple tree, black against the sky. All scraps of joy leave me. This is no celebration. Mary, French Peter and I look at each other and – I am sure – see only dust and bones. We are all stung and instantly infected with a fear so dark and heavy that it feels as though death rides beside us in the cart.

The wheels stop. The crowd, cheering seconds before, quietens. A young woman, heavy with child, throws herself at French Peter, sobbing. Then a small boy starts up some truly awful lament on the pipes. If ever anyone deserved to hang, I think, then natural justice would choose him over me for his crimes against music.

We step down from the cart. I am weak and Mary holds me up. I scan the crowd filling the wooden seats rigged up on a stand for the gentry so they may get a better view. Look us in the eye as our necks snap goodbye. Pretty women, faces lathered in make-up, hold their handkerchiefs to their noses. Their beaus, with wigs as high as heaven and coats that put my own to shame, sit beside them. All pointing at us, laughing, waiting to see us swing. I turn away and meet the executioner's gaze. He is a broad and heavy-set man, and I wonder if the killing weighs against his soul, or maybe he tells himself the story that we are all monsters and truly deserve our dispatch.

One lady laughs, and I look back to the rows of seats stretching up into the sky. Elizabeth Stapleton, sat arm-in-arm with her father, Captain Walker. His eyes are crueller than the executioner's. I hold myself as steady as I can and spit upon the ground. He smiles at me. If I could be a ghost, I tell myself, then I will come back and make their lives more miserable than my last months in Newgate.

The Ordinary begins his prayers for our souls and a Roman priest chants in the Latin tongue for Mary, who is Irish, and swings a metal ball which trails incense, a heady, dreamy, sickly smell that makes my senses giddy. The sobbing is louder now.

A cry of: 'For shame to hang a woman and a boy!'

An echo: 'Shame! A shame.' A rotten turnip head whistles close to the executioner's ear. He ignores it, and holds the ropes like an armful of snakes that will suddenly spring to life and wrap us in their coils. I feel my knees buckle, but take a deep breath. I stand at the foot of a small wooden ladder, my last ascent.

The executioner rigs up the ropes and the nooses hang like empty hoops. I try not to shake, and close my eyes.

'To Cato Hopkins!' a shout rings out. 'The Nest of Vipers send you their regards!'

I open them. I'd swear the voice was Ezra Spinoza's. I look for him but the crowd is like one mass of people pressed close together. Then something moves: a boy darts through the crowd, shiny brown hair tied back under a battered three-cornered hat. I know that hat. That's no boy, never! I know that girl. The rope is placed round my neck. The incense makes my head swim ... I must be seeing things.

The Ordinary leans close. 'The diamonds, boy, the diamonds. Be quick, be quick.'

I look again. The boy pulls the hat down over her face.

The Ordinary is growling now. 'I said, the *diamonds*.'

I lean close to answer.

Then another sound, a voice I don't know. A scream from the stands.

'My purse! It's gone!' One shriek follows another.

The Ordinary leans aside and whispers to the executioner. I don't hear what is said. I am staring at the girl's mouth, and even though I wear the devil's rope necklace, I feel a smile as broad as the Thames cross my face. I hold myself upright. I will die like a man. I will die proud and tall for the world, for Addeline to see.

Then there's a sudden creaking, groaning noise from the wooden stands and we all watch open-mouthed. We are staring – Mary Cut and Come Again, French Peter, the executioner, the Ordinary and all the London flash mob come for a free show – as the whole stand collapses like a house of cards. Wigs, hats, dresses come tumbling down to earth, as petticoats, slippers, fans and gloves fly in all directions. Captain Walker's face is fury, Lady Elizabeth's mouth makes as wide an 'O' as an open noose. So much screaming. This, I imagine, is hell come to London.

We are all smiling now, we who are to die. I look from one to another, then to the boy in the crowd, but she is gone. A dream, a ghost. I hope we will be ghosts together.

'Cato, Cato, quickly. Run!' The ghost whispers in my ear and her breath is not cold – clammy but warm. My whole body tingles, comes alive. The ghost has cut the rope.

'Run!' she says, and I try but my legs give way and buckle, once, twice, again. French Peter has already vanished. Mary gone an instant later. Time seems to have stretched into a gliding, slowed-down dance. The magistrate's men shout and the noise of them is drowned by the screams of the gentry.

They are in two minds: help the gentry or stop us criminals. I feel as if I am moving under water. Pushing through the heavy air, I cannot move. The executioner has seen me, and his eyes narrow as he starts towards us.

Then Addeline puts her shoulder under mine and pulls me through the crowd, which parts and closes behind us like the Red Sea before Moses in the Bible. We are cheered and whistled along, the crowd more excited to see me free than to see us all hang. And then ahead I see a sight I have seen a thousand times in dreams. Sam and Jack on either side of their sedan chair, scuffing their slippers, ready to break into a run. A run for me.

'He's gone! The boy is gone!' I know Captain Walker's shout and hear Addeline's reply.

'Quick sharp, boys, the devil sees us!'

I turn back and see the man's face, a mask of anger, nearing with every step, knocking men, women, children out of his way with blows from his silver-topped cane. Surely any moment I will feel his breath against my cheek! A woman steps out of the crowd just behind him. She is in widow's clothes and veiled. She waves a brickmaker's bat and yells so loud a banshee would protest. In one instant she lifts it, swings it, then Addeline pulls me round before I see the blow. Behind me I hear the bat connect with bone and know the devil Walker will not follow any more.

As I am bundled inside Sam and Jack's chair, I take in the faded brocade and leather interior, and before I know it, the rocking and swaying of the chair and the complete and utter comfort – compared to my more recent lodgings – have lulled my soul. I close my eyes and give in to the gentle mirror of death that is only sleep.

15. A Yellow House in Bath, Michaelmas Day

I HAVE PINCHED myself so often my arm is sore, but I have not yet woken up from what is the sweetest dream.

Mother Hopkins has indeed found a good yellow house, and Jack and Sam have a fine two-wheeler in the coach house and an Arabian so black and shiny you can see your face in her sides. And we are no longer Hopkins here, but Staples, in honour of the diamonds that have provided for our new life.

'Those diamonds made us safe, Cato,' Mother says. 'And you have paid a heavy price. But life is good, and you here makes it one thousand times better. I would not leave any one of my chickens to rot in Newgate, or see them go to hell.' She hugs me tight against her even though I protest. And I know that any questions about my provenance or her history can wait until judgement day for all I care.

And everyone is kind to me, even Bella, who has Jack's ring on her finger and his child in her belly. She says: 'If you'd have gone to heaven on a rope, we'd have called my boy here Cato.' She pats her stomach.

Which is, I think, the nicest thing she has ever said to me.

I cannot recall much of the journey from London, only to say that we went west by river first and then by carriage. I was weak but my appetite returned speedily and now the thought of rat has long since ceased to make my mouth water.

Mother has called a party for me on Michaelmas, to welcome me home. Addeline sends me to fetch the cob nuts and fruit for the party and she says I'm not to come back until six. She says it is a surprise.

When I return, Quarmy is in the hall with his fiddle and we embrace like brothers. He is contrite. 'Accept my apology, please, Cato.'

'It is done. A thousand times over!' I say honestly.

And we go into the hall. There is Mother and Bella with Jack and Sam. Quarmy strikes up a tune, 'The Thames Flows Sweetly', and then I feel behind my eyes a pricking sensation. I think of The Vipers and the sounds of laughter by the fire and the streets running down from Covent Garden to the river, and I have to blink and look away.

Then a girl enters, a beautiful, small-boned, brown-haired girl wearing a dress of the palest grey silk that matches exactly the colour of her eyes. And I know I must have been intoxicated by the Roman incense, for there is no way Addeline could ever be mistaken for a boy.

And we dance, and I don't want the music to ever stop.

Postscript

THE TYBURN DISASTER

It is now known that person or persons of ill fame had deliberately, and with evil intent, sawed through the struts of the stand at Tyburn, causing it to collapse and leaving several ladies with bruised ribs, turned ankles and severe hysterics. The Lady Sarah Whippswill also lost her purse, containing a guinea piece.

One, Martha Cotton, a pie-seller of Paddington, swears on oath that the previous evening when she was returning from Shepherd's Market in Mayfair, she saw a widow woman all in black encouraging two young men to set about the stands with some kind of hacksaw.

In the ensuing confusion following the stand's collapse, the criminals awaiting the just sentence of Her Majesty's law took it upon themselves to escape.

Captain Walker, an elderly gentleman of good heart, gave chase but lost the Hopkins boy in the mob, and indeed suffered himself an injury to the forehead of which he has since quite recovered.

The mob were said to be led by the same aforementioned 'fierce widow woman all in black', who stirred up and inflamed the crowd to such a degree that they turned upon the magistrate's men and robbed several more of the ladies and gentlemen who had attended the hanging in good faith. She has not been found and it may be imagined that she was, in fact, no woman at all, but some foreign agitator in women's dress.

'French' Peter Villeneuve was later re-arrested in Spitalfields in the company of a young lady of ill repute. The crone commonly called Mary Cut and Come Again has been sighted in Chelmsford and thereabouts.

Anyone with any information on the whereabouts of the Negro boy called Cato Hopkins, or the Stapleton diamonds, should inform Captain Walker of Greenwich or the Marquess of Byfield, lately of St James, now also of Greenwich. There is a most generous reward for any information that will lead to his capture.

Extra!

Extra!

READ ALL ABOUT IT!

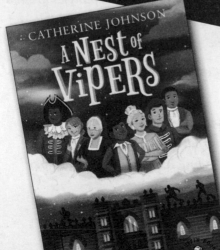

CATHERINE JOHNSON

A NEST OF VIPERS

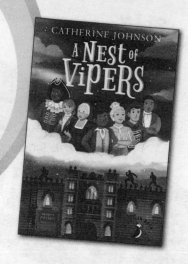

© Eve Carreño

1962	*Born in London*
1967	*Goes to Tetherdown Primary School in north London*
1973	*Attends Henrietta Barnett School in north London*
1979	*Studies film at St Martin's School of Art in London, and works making short films and pop videos*
1989	*Helps a film company buy a pony, Spangles, which is kept at Hackney City Farm and then Kentish Town City Farm. Catherine rides Spangles around London Fields, Victoria Park and – in a childhood dream come true – Hampstead Heath*
1993	*Catherine's first book,* The Last Welsh Summer, *is published*
1999	*Landlocked is published and chosen as one of IBBY's (the International Board of Books for Young People) 'White Ravens' in a round-up of best books of the year*

2004	Co-writes the highly acclaimed feature film Bullet Boy
2007	Becomes a full-time writer
2008	A Nest of Vipers is published by Corgi; Arctic Hero, the true story of African-American explorer Matthew Henson, is also published
2013	Sawbones is published by Walker Books and wins the Young Quills Award for best historical fiction for 12+ the following year. Moves to the seaside in Hastings, Kent
2015	The Curious Tale of the Lady Caraboo is published and nominated for the highly prestigious Carnegie Medal and the YA Book Prize in 2016
2018	Freedom is published by Scholastic and is nominated for the Carnegie Medal; Race to the Frozen North is published by Barrington Stoke
2019	Is made a Fellow of the Royal Society of Literature; Freedom wins the Little Rebel Award (a children's book prize set up by the Association of Radical Booksellers)
2020	Freedom is chosen by IBBY as its honour list title. Adapts Miranda Kaufman's award-winning non-fiction book Black Tudors for TV
2021	Queen of Freedom is shortlisted for the Jhalak Prize

INTERESTING FACTS

When Catherine was young she loved the Sunday-afternoon serials on TV, especially the historical dramas, but when she came to play out the stories in the playground at school there was never anyone that represented people like her. After she grew up and became a writer, she started to create characters that represented herself and although the people in her historical novels are made up, they are always based on truth.

Catherine has been a Writer in Residence at Holloway Prison, a Royal Literary Fund Writing Fellow at the London Institute and has mentored writers in Africa for the British Council.

GUESS WHO?

A '. . . Me and Sam, as things stand, we can make an honest wage.'

B I would be swinging in the wind, dancing the devil's own jig on the end of a noose.

C 'You will find out in a year or so that broken hearts are ten a penny!'

D 'Captain Walker promised my mother he'd make me a free man.'

E 'Cato, Cato, quickly. Run!'

F 'You know my ways by now, Jack, and I am not to be tainted with honest money! Never!'

WORDS GLORIOUS WORDS!

We often come across new or unfamiliar words when we are reading. Here are a few unusual words you'll find in this Puffin book. Did you spot any others?

cant *the old word for the secret language of thieves*

carriage and pair *a two-horse drawn carriage*

cod *fake, something that is not genuine, intended to amuse people by looking or sounding like the real thing*

coney catchers *thieves – those who preyed on easy targets in the streets of London. 'Con men' in today's language*

costermonger *A person who sells goods, especially fruit and vegetables, from a handcart in the street*

cutpurse *a pickpocket or thief*

dullard *a stupid, unimaginative person*

flummery *excessive fuss or flattery*

fustian *a type of heavy cloth woven from cotton*

lays *tricks or scams*

manteau *a loose gown or cloak worn by women in the seventeenth and eighteenth centuries*

mark *an old slang term for a person who is to be the target of a scam*

nabob *a rich and powerful person*

provenance *where something or someone first came from*

sarabande *a dance that originated in Central America in the sixteenth century*

shammy *a cloth made from leather (also known as a chamois leather)*

QUIZ

1 **What is the name of the ship that 'vanished'?**

a) *The* Favourite

b) *The* Lost

c) *The* Titanic

2 **Who had Sam Caesar escaped from?**

a) *Lady Godwin*

b) *Juno*

c) *Captain Walker*

3 **What jewels were NOT on Prince Quarmy's ship?**

a) *Rubies*

b) *Diamonds*

c) *Jade*

4 *Which country is Prince Quarmy from?*

a) *The Republic of Benin*

b) *The Kingdom of Wakanda*

c) *The Kingdom of Bonny*

5 *Who did Bella pretend to be?*

a) *Ekaterina, Queen of Moscow*

b) *Ekaterina, Countess of Pskoff*

c) *Arabella, Princess of Petersburg*

6 *What year did the heist happen?*

a) *1712*

b) *1725*

c) *1803*

7 *What prison is Cato held at?*

a) *Newgate Prison*

b) *Oldgate Prison*

c) *Frontgate Prison*

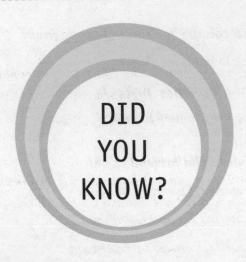

DID YOU KNOW?

Just like today, everyone who visited London during the 1700s was excited by the noise, *the* crowds *and the* busy atmosphere. *But, unlike today, the city of London was neither charming or clean – in fact, it absolutely* stank!

After the Great Fire *of 1666, which destroyed most of the city, London was built in a hasty and haphazard manner. There was great poverty and many people lived in filthy ramshackle houses, squashed together and divided up to cram in as many families as possible. The streets became a* maze of narrow, dark, smelly alleyways *that were excellent cover for pickpockets and other dangerous criminals.*

London was filled with the smell of horse manure and rotting rubbish, and raw sewage ran along the city streets in open drains. Many people would empty their chamber pots straight out of their windows on to the road below!

Newgate Prison, first built in medieval times, existed until 1902 and was finally demolished in 1904 so that the new Central Criminal Court, which opened in 1907 (known as the Old Bailey), could be built on the site.

IN THIS YEAR

2008 Fact Pack

What else was happening in the world when A Nest of Vipers was first published?

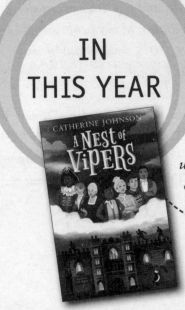

*China hosts the **Summer Olympics** in Beijing. The American swimmer **Michael Phelps** wins a record eight Gold medals, while Jamaican sprinter **Usain Bolt** sets world records in the 100m, the 200m and the 4 x 100m relay races – the first man to do so in one Olympics.*

*Scientists discover that **Stonehenge** is older than originally thought by nearly 500 years, and therefore likely to have been erected in 3000 BC.*

Barak Obama becomes the forty-fourth US president – the first African-American to be elected to this office.

The UK experiences its largest **earthquake**, measuring 5.2 on the Richter scale, in twenty-five years.

The UK *prime minister* is Gordon Brown.

PUFFIN
WRITING
TIPS

Write a description of your home town as if you were arriving there for the very first time.

Change your scenery and go and see something you've never seen before.

Catherine says:

Keep a notebook. But if you're not the notebook type that's fine too.

Write that thing down before you go to bed. You won't remember in the morning.

Don't use words you don't need. Less is more. Make sure every word matters.

A PUFFIN BOOK

stories that last a lifetime

Ever wanted a friend who could take you to magical realms, talk to animals or help you survive a shipwreck? Well, you'll find them all in the **A PUFFIN BOOK** collection.

A PUFFIN BOOK will stay with you **forever**. Maybe you'll read it again and again, or perhaps years from now you'll suddenly **remember** the moment it made you **laugh** or **cry** or simply see things **differently**. Adventurers **big** and **small**, rebels out to **change** their world, even a mouse with a **dream** and a spider who can spell – these are the characters who make **stories** that last a **lifetime**.

Whether you love animal tales, war stories or want to know what it was like growing up in a different time and place, the **A PUFFIN BOOK** collection has a story for you – you just need to decide where you want to go next . . .

A Puffin Book can take you to amazing places.

WHERE WILL YOU GO?

#PackAPuffin